Just One Night

Misty Payton

DEDICATION

This book is dedicated to my wonderful and amazing kids. Ricky & Chelby I love you both more than words can say. I believe you can do anything you set your minds to do. I hope this helps you to know that no matter the time or place you can try new things. Never be afraid to do new things and set new goals each day. Mama loves you to the moon and back.

Anderson's Bed & Breakfast is a beautiful Bed & Breakfast located on an island off the coast of South Carolina. Sheyenne "Nicole" has been working as the Events Manger at her family own Bed & Breakfast for the last five years. She's been happy but there's just one thing haunting her dreams at night.

It's been five years since Nicole met Trent while on a ladies trip to New York with her two best friends. Nicole has dreamed about their night together and what it would feel like to be in Trent's arms again. Just one night and now she feels like a part of her heart is missing. Nicole and Trent's connection was more than a physical one. Yes, she would have to admit that sex with Trent was amazing but it was more than that. Nicole has regretted never getting Trent's full name that night. Trent has become the man who lives only in her dreams. Nicole left a part of her heart with Trent and no matter how she tries she's unable to fill that missing part of her heart.

The Bed & Breakfast is a wonderful place for destination weddings. While meeting with a new client who is thinking of using the island for her wedding, Nicole's heart stops when the man who walks in during the meeting is the man she has dreamed about for the last five years.

Was Nicole only ever meant to have just one night or could there be something more for them in the future?

CONTENTS

Special Thanks

I would like to thank God for blessing me with the ability to put this story together. Corey, Daphne, Jasmine, and Lori thank you for reading my story as it was being created. Your advice and guidance helped me create the best story I could. Y'all were amazing sound boards that helped me know I was on the right path.

Chapter 1

      Running on the beach at sunrise has always been my favorite time of the day. The cool morning breeze is filled with salt and fresh ocean smells. It gives me the time to forget and remember the past, present, and hopes for the future. I'm able to clear my mind for the day ahead. I learned years ago that running was my way of relaxing and letting go. "Shy, slow down", Sasha tries to yell. She is breathing hard from our morning run. "Come on Shy we've already ran five miles." You're trying to kill me." She manages to say between breaths. What are you running from? Is always her next question when I've completely zoned out. My mind always goes back to one single thought. I come to a stop and shrug my shoulders as I turn to check on my younger sister. Sasha is sitting on the sand near the water. Her strawberry blonde hair is in a ponytail and she is dressed in black yoga pants with a red sports bra. "Sash you didn't have to run the whole five miles with me," I snicker at her. She cuts her beautiful green eyes at me and gives me the death glare. This causes me to laugh harder. I'm two years older than Sasha so her glares do nothing to me. I've mastered the art of ignoring Sasha's glares but, sometimes the looks cause me to break out into laughter. Sasha looks away when I start laughing.

While still laughing, I walk over and sit down next to her. The damp sand is cool to the touch but by mid-morning that will change. "Sorry Sash, I wasn't trying to kill you. You know how I get when I'm running." She looks up to me and smiles "Yes I do, but I was hoping you would take it easy on me." Sasha has just returned from a two week work related leisure trip. Sasha toured Italy looking for new dishes that we could feature at the Bed & Breakfast our family owns off the coast of South Carolina. "I'll try to take it easy next time" I tell her. By now she is giggling with me. "You know it's time to head back we have a lot of work today. Dad has several new clients coming." I tell her as I lean over to give her a small hug. She nods in agreement. As I push myself up, I feel the sand between my fingers. I enjoy the smooth feel of the sand as I dig my fingers in. Once I'm standing, I reach my hand out to help Sasha up. "Come on Sash, we'll walk the last half mile back to the house." On our walk back, Sasha tells me about the many different restaurants and villages she visited while in Italy. I listen and respond at the correct times but I'm paying more attention to the seagulls flying above the waves. They are trying to catch their breakfast as the waves roll up the beach. Sasha and I grew up on this beautiful beach and no matter how many times I've came here I'm still amazed by the beauty. Fifteen minutes later, we've reached the Bed & Breakfast and we head toward our homes.

Our Parents live in the private living quarters attached to the Bed & Breakfast. They decided it was more cost effective to move when Sasha left for culinary school. Sasha and I live in two additional houses near the main house. Sasha lives in our childhood home and I live in the home our grandparents had built when they first moved to the island. She and I had both homes renovated and modernized, but at the same time leaving a lot of the original structure. Our homes have a lot of family history and add to the beauty of the Bed & Breakfast. Sasha and I help our parents run Anderson's Bed & Breakfast. The Bed & Breakfast has been in our family for sixty years. Our grandparents, Paul and Sally Anderson saw the potential this small secluded island had. Because of the beauty and secluded location, my grandparents knew people would pay to stay in a location completely away from their everyday life. With this in mind they built a twenty room Colonial Mansion. The island is located off the coast of South Carolina. The only way to access the island is by a short boat ride from the small town of Madison. We're able to provide our guests the privacy to enjoy their time away from their busy life.

My sister Sasha graduated at the top of her culinary class and is considered a top chef among her peers. She has managed the restaurant and kitchen at the Bed & Breakfast for the last three years. Anderson's has been rated in the top five of all Bed & Breakfast restaurants in the United States for the past two years. I manage and oversee all events held at Anderson's Bed & Breakfast. Our parents, John & Lilly Andrews handle the business side of the operation. Dad is over scheduling and meetings with potential guest. Mom is a certified CPA, so she takes care of the accounting needs. We work together like a well-oiled machine and due to our ability to work as a team the Bed & Breakfast has received several awards.

Chapter 2

I make it home and head to the bathroom to get ready for work. Next to running on the beach, standing in my large shower as the double showerhead sprays the hot water down on me is one of my favorite things to do. The hot water helps relax my tighten muscles from the vigorous run. I step out of the shower to get ready for the day and wrap a large cozy towel around me. I reach for another and begin to towel dry my long auburn hair. My hair is naturally wavy so I plan to leave it down. I check to see what the weather forecast is before I get dressed. It's going to be a cool breezy day. Knowing the weather I step into the walk-in closet attached to my bathroom. I take down my favorite pale green blouse and dress slacks. The green blouse accents the green in my eyes perfectly. The light colors of the outfit look great against my olive skin tone, hazel eyes and reddish brown hair. Since I'll be meeting with new clients today, I decide to add a light amount of foundation to my face and color my eyelids with brown, olive green, and a touch of gold eye shadow. After adding eyeliner and mascara my eyes are shining back at me from the mirror. The rosy blush and lip gloss are my finishing touch.

As I'm slipping on my cream sandals my phone beeps. I glance down to see my dad's name on the caller id. Dad has scheduled several new clients today and a few return guests. Reviewing the text message, I see dad also sent the schedule containing all of today's appointments. Our first appointments have used the Bed & Breakfast in the past so I'll let him handle those few guests by himself. Returning guests are familiar with our accommodations and require less attention from me. The returning guests are coming back for a few days of fun and relaxation. The Bed & Breakfast has a wide range of options for our guest to indulge in and have fun. After I review the meeting schedule for today, I slide my phone into the front pocket and leave the house to have breakfast at the main house.

I hear laughing and talking as I walk up the steps to the private kitchen attached to the main kitchen of the Bed & Breakfast. Every morning, mom, dad, Sasha, and I meet for breakfast. This allows us to have family time together without worrying about work. This morning I hear Sash telling mom and dad "Shy was trying to kill me during our morning run." I walk in the door and see them sitting at the breakfast bar. Mom is wearing a creamy white sundress that looks amazing next to her olive skin. Dad is in his usual khaki pants and a white button up shirt. "No, Sash I wasn't but I can't help that you decided to be lazy during your trip." I say laughing. "Good morning mom and dad, how are y'all doing this morning?" "Good morning honey, we're good. So you had a wonderful run this morning?" My mom asks. "Yes ma'am I did." "Morning." I hear my dad say over his cup of coffee while he is reading the morning paper. I walk over and give him a kiss on the cheek as I grab a bowl from the counter for my grits. This morning Ms. Betty Ann, our cook, has prepared grits, bacon, and toast for us.

I take a seat next to dad at the breakfast bar. We talk and laugh as we enjoy our breakfast together. "Okay dad, I'm going to let you handle the meetings with our return guest. I will join you for the new clients." I inform dad. "Sure darling that's fine with me. The new clients need more attention since they haven't decided if they will use our location for their parties. We have a Sweet Sixteen party, a couple of weddings, and even an office retreat." Dad replies. "Great I'll see you at 9:45 for the first appointment." I tell him as I get up from my seat next to him, rinse my bowl out in the sink, and put it in the dishwasher. "Thank you Ms. Betty Ann, breakfast was terrific as always." I tell her as I place a kiss on her cheek. "You're welcome sweet cakes." Ms. Betty Ann replies. Ms. Betty Ann has been cooking for us for as long as I can remember.

I walk from the kitchen to the front of the house where my office is located. I need to check the schedules and make sure we have enough employees scheduled to work today. Summer happens to be our busiest time of the year. Normally we're booked up through the months of June, July, and August. Construction began a few months ago to add additional rooms to the Bed & Breakfast so we can accommodate more guests. The additional rooms will be ready to rent out in the next two months. The new addition will be ideal for wedding parties. The additional housing is away from the main house in a secluded area which gives the guest added privacy. After reviewing today's schedule, I decide to go and catch up with Megan. Megan Jones, one of my best friends, is the Massage Therapist at the Spa located at the Bed & Breakfast. Megan trained to be a massage therapist as soon as we graduated from High School and has been working here ever since. I walk over to the spa to check on how Megan's doing today. I see Megan opening the door to her office so I call out. "Hi Meg, how are you this morning?" Megan turns and gives me a big smile. "Hi Shy, I'm great. Just checking the schedule to see how many clients I have today." She walks over to her desk and pulls up today's schedule. "So how many do you have booked today?" I ask. "So far there are three one hour massages and four thirty minute massages," Megan replies. "So you have a full day that's great." I reply as I sit in the chair next to her desk. Megan turns the chair to face me and leans back to get comfortable. I sit and chat with Megan until her first appointment arrives. Megan and I talk about her husband, kids, and how her parents are enjoying retirement. We make plans for supper one night soon as I'm leaving her office.

On the way back to my office I decide to check on other areas of the Bed & Breakfast. Over the years we've added additional rooms and activities for our guest. When I took over as manager of activities and events, we decided to open our services to the public. This was a good business decision that it helped spread the word about the Bed & Breakfast. When we installed a new computer system, we also updated our website. The website allows guest and non-guest to schedule appointments for the spa, hair salon, horseback riding, hiking, and several other water sports.

Chapter 3

My phone chirps to remind me of the meeting with Mrs. Green and her soon to be sixteen year old daughter, Amber. Amber wants a Sweet Sixteen Birthday party filled with glam and pampering for her and ten of her closest friends. I've already put the party plan together and Sasha has the food list ready for Mrs. Green and Amber to review. I walk to my office to retrieve the proposal I have ready for them. When I pass the receptionist desk, Ashley informs me that Mrs. Green and Amber have arrived early. I walk into dad's office to see if he is ready. "Dad" I call as I enter his office. "Mrs. Green and her daughter have arrived early, can I go ahead and bring them in." I ask "Yes, sugar you can." He says as he comes through the door of the adjoining office where my mom works. He takes a seat at his desk. I walk back to retrieve Mrs. Green and Amber from the reception area and lead them to my father's office.

Forty five minutes later we have set the date for Amber's Sweet Sixteen Birthday party. Amber fell in love with all the party ideas Sasha and I had put together.

The rest of the day passes just as fast as the morning did. Dad and I met with the representatives from Joe's Automotive to discuss the option of them using our location for their next office retreat. We were also able to help the newly engaged Mr. White and Ms. Johnson decide on a wedding date. All in all this has been a productive morning. It's one o'clock and the next appointment isn't til 2:30. So I decide to have a quick bite to eat. I grab lunch from the kitchen and take it back to my desk. If we land the next client it will put the Anderson's Bed & Breakfast on a new level. I review the proposal Sash and I put together one more time while I finish eating my sandwich. I feel very confident that this proposal will amaze the client. Nikki Clouse, the Bride to be, is the daughter of the well-known fashion designer Natalee Clouse. Clouse Designs have been worn at red carpet events by A-list celebrities for the past five years. I tried searching the internet for any information that could assist with our proposal but was unable to locate information on Nikki and her fiancé. Nikki Clouse has been able to keep her personal life out of the media even though her mother is a famous Designer. The privacy we offer at Anderson's Bed & Breakfast is the main reason Nikki is interested in our location.

Since Sasha will be joining dad and I for the meeting, I walk over to her office and make sure there isn't anything else we need to add or update on the proposal. I knock on the door of Sash's office and hear her tell me to come in. "Hi Sash, is there anything new I need to add to our proposal before the Clouse meeting?" I ask. She looks up from the paperwork she is working on and nods her head no. "I think we've added enough catering and additional menu options already. We don't want to overdo it." She adds while standing to straighten her black knee length skirt. The white button up blouse makes her looks professional. Normally Sasha is busy in the kitchen working on the menu for the restaurant or helping prepare food for the catering. So it's really nice to see her out of her normal cooking uniform.

It's 2:15 when Sasha and I enter dad's office to see dad talking with a beautiful lady with long blonde hair. Nikki Clouse arrived early for the appointment. Dad looks up as Sasha and I walk into his office. He stands and introduces us. "Ms. Clouse these two beautiful ladies are my daughters." Dad gestures to Sasha. "This beautiful one here is Sasha. Sasha is a Chef and she manages the restaurant and catering for the Bed & Breakfast." Sasha reaches out, shakes Nikki's hand and tells her it's nice to meet her. "And this beautiful one is Sheyenne." I take Nikki's extend hand and shake it. I tell her how much of a pleasure it is to meet her. Dad explains to Nikki that I'm the manager of activities and events held at the Bed & Breakfast. "It's a pleasure to meet you both." Nikki states. Just as Sasha and I start walking toward the chairs next to dad's desk, Ashley calls over the intercom to let us know Mr. Hudson is on his way in. Dad tells Ashley thank you. Nikki looks really happy to hear Mr. Hudson has arrived. Mr. Hudson must be the groom. I hear the door open so I turn to greet Mr. Hudson and stop dead in my tracks. Time seems to stop as soon as my eyes meet Mr. Hudson's blue eyes. Nikki hops up and gives him a huge hug before she introduces him to everyone in the office. I come back to my senses just as Nikki starts introducing me. "Xzavier this is Sheyenne Anderson. She is the Events Manager here at the Bed & Breakfast. Sheyenne this is Xzavier Hudson." Xzavier reaches out takes my hand in his and I feel the hairs on my neck stand. I feel a need and an ache that I haven't felt in years. "It's wonderful to meet you all." he says as he takes the seat next to Nikki.

Dad starts explaining the history and why Anderson's Bed & Breakfast is the best choice for the wedding ceremony. While dad is talking I feel Xzavier's eyes on me and I do my best to keep my emotions in check. I can't allow myself to show just how much seeing him has affected me. Xzavier showed no emotion when I was introduced. I wonder if seeing me has had any effect on him. I take over explaining the privacy Anderson's would offer them for their wedding ceremony. I asked if they would like to see the locations where the wedding ceremony could be held. Nikki is excited to take a tour around the grounds. First, I take them down to the beach location we specifically use for wedding ceremonies. "This beach" I tell them "has beautiful white sand that sparkles like diamonds in the sun light. The beach also has a wonderful rock ledge with a huge cavern entrance." Once we get to the beach I hear Nikki gasp at the beautiful site before her. "Xzavier this is gorgeous." Nikki states. "Yes this place is amazing." Xzavier replies. "Can I take a picture to show my mom? This place would also be wonderful for a swimsuit photo shoot." Nikki states. I nod that it was fine for her to take pictures.

I lead the group to the second possible wedding ceremony location. We've created this beautiful flower garden filled with flowers of all colors and sizes. Nikki is just as excited to see this location. She takes more pictures to show her mother. Xzavier and Nikki have walked away from us to look around. When they are out of hearing distance, Sasha walks over to me. "You looked like you saw a ghost when Xzavier walked into the office. What is wrong?" She says low enough dad can't hear her. I turn and face her. "I'll have to explain later." I tell her. Sasha looks like she wants to ask more questions but decides to stop when Nikki and Xzavier return. We start walking back to dad's office as Sasha explains the different menu options available for the wedding reception. Nikki and Sasha are talking back and forth about the different items on the menus. I barely hear them because I'm mentally fighting to keep my emotions in check. I haven't had this many emotions to deal with in years. It's driving me crazy. "Hey Shy, did you hear me?" Dad asked. "Sorry, no I'm trying to make sure we've covered everything. What did you ask?" I ask dad. "Do you have the expected completion date for the new additions?" He asks. "Yes, those should be finished in the next month." I answer.

Dad turns to Nikki and relays my answer. Nikki looks at Xzavier to ask what he thinks about having the wedding here. "I believe it would be an excellent place for the wedding." He answers. "How many people can the two new buildings accommodate?" Nikki asks. "Each building has enough rooms for forty people, but there is also a single occupancy cabin a little farther behind the two buildings." I tell her. "Wonderful the wedding is two months away so that should allow enough time for the construction on all three locations to be completed. I've decided I would love to have my wedding ceremony here." Nikki tells dad. "We're extremely happy that you have decided to use our location for your wedding." Dad tells her while shaking her hand.

As we make our way back to dad's office, mom joined us on the walk back. Sash and I leave mom and dad with Nikki and Xzavier so they can discuss the billing side of the agreement. Before Sasha and I leave Nikki tells us that we'll be working with her wedding planner to make sure we have everything setup correctly. Nikki decided to have the wedding at the beach right at sunset and the reception will be held in the garden. "That is a wonderful idea." I tell Nikki. "The two of you will have a magical wedding." I tell them. They both pause and it looks like they're going to say something but my cell phone starts ringing. "Excuse me

I've got to take this call." I walk into the hallway and answer my phone. As I finish my phone call Sasha walks up behind me. I can tell by the look on her face, she wants to finish the conversation we started in the garden. "Let's go to your office and I'll explain everything to you." I say before she can even open her mouth to ask me the first question. Sasha nods her head in agreement and we walk to her office in dead silence. I'm trying to put all the thoughts in my head in order so I can explain why seeing Xzavier has affected me so much. It has been years since I've felt like I've been on a train ride that doesn't end.

When we reach Sasha's office, I close the office door and turn to see that Sasha is staring at me waiting for answers. I look down to my trembling hands and simply say. "I was looking into the blue eyes of the man I thought I'd never see again. Those blue eyes still have the same effect on me now as they did the very first time I looked into them five years ago." I look up to see the shock on Sasha's face. The only words Sasha is managing to say are "Oh Shit! You have got to be kidding me." I stand there and shake my head as I feel the tears fill my eyes. I've manage to hold myself together up to this point but I can't do it anymore. "Are you sure Xzavier is Trent. It has been five years since you last saw him." Sasha asks. "Yes, I will never forget him or the way he made me feel. That is the man I fell in love with." I answer as I put my head in my hands. Thinking of Trent and Nikki getting married is tearing me apart.

Chapter 4

Five years ago.........Nicole

I'm in New York on a girls retreat with Brandy and
Megan, my two best friends. Brandy Holmes and Megan
Lowes have been my closest friends since grade school.
We've been there for each other when life had been good
and when it was bad. Megan is getting married in a few
weeks so we decided to take one last trip to celebrate her
last few weeks of freedom. We've been in New York for four
days and this is our last night there. We thought it would
be fun to bar hop our last night in New York. Our final
nightclub of the night is the Skyline that is located on the
top floor of our hotel. The Nasser Hotel is one of the newly
renovated hotels in New York and the Skyline nightclub is
an added incentive for people staying at the hotel. If you're
a guest of the hotel the coverage charge to enter the

nightclub is waved. Your room key is used for all transactions in the nightclub. All charges from the nightclub are added to your hotel bill and paid at time you check out. The Skyline is packed to the max. There are people dancing, drinking, and sitting at the tables or booths located around the club. The bars are located in each corner; sitting areas are between the bars and the dance floor in the center. The Skyline transports you back in time to the 1940s. All the staff are dressed in the clothing from the era which helps add to the coolness of this bar. The DJ is playing a variety of dance music and the dance floor is packed with people dancing along with the beat. Every bar we've been to has been nice but this one is the best so far. Brandy, Megan, and I are sitting at the bar and the bartender has placed a shot of whiskey in front of me. "Take the shot. Take the shot. Take the shot." Brandy and Megan start chanting. I look over at them and smile as I tip my head back and down the shot. The whiskey burns as it goes down and I hear both girls yell. "That's our girl." "It's time to dance so let's get on the dance floor and shake our money makers." I yell to them over the music. As we get up from the bar I notice these three guys sitting at a table near the bar. The guys have been watching us for the past thirty minutes. One of the guys is leaning over the table in talking to the guy that has his back to us. Just as we pass the table the guy turns around and looks up at me. I look into his beautiful clear blue eyes. His blue eyes remind me how the ocean looks when the sun shines down on it at sunrise. The whiskey I just drank can't match the feeling I have from looking into those blue eyes. He smiles at me and the sparkle in his eyes becomes brighter. I could lose myself in his eyes. I'm forced to break eye contact when Megan grabs my hand and leads me to the dance floor.

Brandy, Megan, and I were the lead dancers for our high school dance line. Dancing is a love of ours. We still get together and dance as a way to stay in shape. As we step on the dance floor Love Game, by Lady Gaga starts blasting through the speakers. This song is one of the many songs we created a dance routine for. We dance in perfect time with each other and the crowd backs away to give us room. As the songs change we change our dance routine as the beat of the next song starts. We've danced together so long that we know how to seamlessly change the dance routine without having to interrupt our dancing. By the end of the next few songs a crowd has gathered around us. Brandy, Megan, and I hear the cheers from the crowd. I look around the crowd and instantly look into those beautiful blue eyes. He's looking me up and down. I get the first chance to check out the body that goes along with the eyes. He's wearing blue jeans that hang low on the hip and a tight blue t-shirt that shows the muscles in his shoulders, chest, and arms. I imagine how it would feel to have those arms wrapped around me. I'm not sure what's come over me because I've never wanted someone as much I want him at this point. I'm filled with the need and desire to have his body move with mine.

I move my eyes up to meet his. He starts walking toward me as if I had called to him. I see the desire and lust in his eyes that match the feelings I'm having. Before I realize it he is standing in front of me, he's a little taller than me so I have to look up so I can look him in the eyes. "Hi. My name is Trent. You're an amazing dancer. Will you dance with me?" I hear him say. "Hi. My name is Nicole and yes I'd love to dance with you." My voice comes out as a whisper but he's close enough that he can hear me. It's hard for me to think when his body is this close to mine. I'm lucky that I remembered to give him my middle name. It's a rule I've had ever since I started going to clubs. I can feel heat from his body and it's causing my body to overheat. Trent takes my hand just as the DJ starts playing Bailando by Enrique Iglesias. Our bodies move in perfect sync with each other like we are made for each other. He is an excellent dancer and he's able to keep up with my every step. I feel his hard and firm muscles as I run my hands down his chest and arms. Trent picks me up and as I slide down the front of him I can feel the hard bulge in his pants. I'm turned on by just the feel of this gorgeous man.

Just as the song is ending Trent lifts me and holds me against him. His body feels amazing against mine and my nipples are hard from being close to him. "Come back to my room with me." He whispers in my ear. It sounded more of a command than an actual question. My breathing has accelerated and I barely manage to answer him back.

"Yes." I whisper back against his lips as I look into his eyes. I knew if I had a chance I could get lost in his blue eyes. Being this close to him is causing my mind and body to short circuit. My want has turned into a burning need to have this man. It's a need, I must give into.

Chapter 5

Trent takes a hold of my hand and begins leading us off the dance floor. He's walking toward the elevator. I tug his hand to get his attention. He stops and turns to face me. "I need to let my friends know I'm leaving. Give me just a minute. I'll meet you at the elevator." I tell Trent. He leans down and gives me a quick kiss on the lips. "Sure but don't take long. I want to feel your body on mine." He says in a soft whisper that causes me to want him more. I walk over to the bar where Brandy and Megan are sitting. I let them know what's going on and that I'll see them in the morning. As I walk away I hear them snicker and say. "Have a great time." I yell. "I plan to." back to them over my shoulder.

I make it to the elevator and Trent is propped up against the wall waiting for me. I take a second to look over his sexy body. He hits the call button for the elevator.

When the elevator arrives we're the only ones on it. As soon as the doors close, Trent gently pushes me up against the wall and picks me up so I can wrap my legs around his waist. I run my hands through his sandy blond hair and kiss him with all the passion and lust I'm feeling. Trent's room happens to be a few floors down, so when the elevator stops he sets me down so I can stand and walk to his room. We barely make it into the room when he has me against the wall kissing me as his hands are massaging my breast. My nipples are so hard that the fabric of my bra is hurting them. It's as if he's reading my mind, he pulls my shirt over my head and removes my bra. Trent picks me up and I wrap my legs around his waist. I feel his hard cock pushing against the seam of his pants. He kisses and nibbles my left nipple while rubbing the right one with his fingers. With every touch I begin to moan and reach for his shirt to remove it. I look him in the eyes and say. "When I lose a piece of clothing so do you." Trent smiles at me and replies. "That sounds like a terrific idea." He kisses his way from the left breast to the right breast and gives it the same attention he did the left breast. He kisses his way back up my neck to my ear and then my lips. Trent carries me to the bed and lays me down with my ass at the edge of the bed. "Nicole I've wanted to taste you ever since I saw you down that shot of whiskey." He tells me as he starts kissing his way to my ear, then down my neck. A soft moan escapes my lips and I run my hands through his hair. Trent is kissing his way down my chest stopping to give my breast more attention. His soft kisses cause me squirm and rub against him. I feel my orgasm building with each kiss and touch. Trent unbuttons my pants and slips them and my lacy underwear down my legs. I hear my pants hit the floor beside the bed and then I feel Trent placing soft kisses around my belly button. I've propped my feet on the side board of the bed to give Trent better access. Trent is on his knees and pushes my legs wide open. This allows him direct access to my throbbing core. He moves between my legs and starts kissing my left thigh. Trent takes the pad of his thumb and begins to rub my nub. The slow circles and slight pressure causes me to release another moan. "You're so soft and wet." He says as he licks my nub and slowly works his way to my entrance. As he slides his tongue in me I release a loud moan. I put my hands in his hair and begin to move my hips in a slow circular motion. Trent is licking and sucking me like I'm the best meal he's ever had. Trent replaces his tongue with two fingers and my hips move in rhythm with his fingers as they're moving in and out of me. He continues to rub my nub with his thumb while his other fingers are rubbing my sensitive core. "Trent I'm about to cum." I manage to moan out just as I feel myself tighten around Trent's fingers and my release comes fast. "Trent continues to slide his fingers in and out me as I come down from my orgasmic high. He removes his fingers and begins to lick and suck my entrance. "So sweet." I hear him say

I'm trying to get my breathing under control when Trent moves up my body to kiss my lips. Trent is lying on top of me and I can feel his hard cock pushing against my sensitive lips. He pushes himself up to stand and helps me sit up. I reach to unbutton his blue jeans. Since I'm still sitting on the bed his waist is eye level. As I slide his pants down his legs his large cock springs free. I lean over to lick the moisture from the tip and down to the base of his cock before he steps out of pants. I stand and make him sit on the bed so I can kneel between his legs. I look up so I can see his reaction as I tell him. "I want to taste you now." I slide my tongue over the tip and suck his cock into my mouth. I hear Trent release a deep moan of pleasure right before he places his hands in my hair. I feel him tighten his grip on my hair as we start to move in rhythm with each other. Trent begins to move his hips up and down as I suck and lick his cock. I glance up to see him watching me and pleasure is written all over his face. I continue to suck, lick, and slide my hand up and down his long swollen cock. I keep sliding my hand up and down his cock so I can glance up to see the expression on his face. Pleasure is written all over his face and by the amount of moans coming from those sexy lips I can tell he's enjoying himself.

Before I'm able to stick his cock back in my mouth, he has grabbed me around the waist and sits me on his lap. We slide back on the bed, I straddle him and I feel the head of his cock at my entrance. The need to feel him inside me has me wet again. I slowly push myself down his cock. I moan louder as each inch goes further inside me. To finally have him inside me sends me over the edge. "Oh my goodness it feels amazing to have you inside me." I manage to say between each moan. I've never experience any feeling like this before. I hear Trent growl with pleasure as I slide his cock further inside me. "Nicole you're so tight and I don't want to hurt you." Trent manages to whisper in my ear. "Don't worry the pleasure I feel out weights the pain." I reply between moans. Trent grabs the back of my head to pull me in for a kiss as I start moving up and down his extremely hard cock. He's so big that it takes a minute for me to accommodate his size. I start with slow up and down movements sliding to the tip and back down. The pleasure takes over and I begin to move faster. Trent is matching my movements. We're moving with the same rhythm we've had all night. It's like our bodies were made for each other. I feel another orgasm building the longer I ride Trent. I use my legs to keep the motion going and I lean closer to kiss him. All of a sudden Trent has flipped us over and he is on top of me. The feel of Trent's body on top of mine while he's inside me is pushing me over the edge. He picks up the rhythm of sliding in and out of me. With each push he's hitting my g spot. "Harder Trent. I want it harder. You won't hurt me. I'm almost there." I manage to tell Trent between moans tell Trent. Trent becomes a wild man when I moan out my need for him to move faster. Trent is moving faster and ramming into me harder. Trent and I cum together at the same time moaning with pleasure as we continue to ride the wave until we have nothing left.

Trent is lying on top of me and his cock is still inside of me. I start rubbing his back and butt and I feel his cock start growing again. He turns his head and places a soft kiss on my lips. Trent is smiling that gorgeous smile and asks. "Are you ready for round two? I can't get enough of your sweet body." I slowly start moving my hips in a circular motion and reply with a soft moan "Yes let's see who will tire out first." Trent chuckles and says. "Baby I'm up for the challenge." He starts moving with me. I have no doubt that this is going to be a long night. I can't get enough of him. Trent's cock grows even harder as we find our rhythm again. With each stroke he is sending me closer to my third orgasm.

Chapter 6

The morning sunshine is coming through the slightly parted curtains. The feel of the warm sunshine on my face wakes me and I realize I'm not in my room. Memories from the night before slowly come back and I enjoy every one of them. When I start to stretch and get out of bed I realize just how sore my body is. Trent and I didn't get enough of each other until sometime in the early morning. By the way my body feels I've used muscles I didn't know I had. I smile because the soreness is a reminder of the sex filled night Trent and I experienced. I've never went to bed with a man without getting to know him first. The only things I know about Trent is his first name and how excellent he is in bed. I reach to the other side of the bed to find Trent isn't there. I slowly get out of bed to go in search of Trent but he isn't anywhere in the room. I happen to glance at the time on my phone. I'm going to be late for my flight back to home if

I don't get going. I grab my pants from the floor, pull them on and go in search of my top that was left by the door. I grab the rest of my items and rush out of the room. I decide to take the stairs since my room is only three floors down from Trent's room. I run down the three floors to enter the hallway where my room is. The run helps loosen my sore muscles. I'm reaching for my room key when Brandy opens the door for me. "There you are." She says to me as I enter the room. "Sorry guys I didn't hear the alarm on my phone and I just woke up." I tell them as I head to the bathroom to take a quick shower. Megan laughs and yells. "You look like you were rode hard and put up wet." I stick my head out the door. "That is basically what happen last night." I reply with a smile. They both break out into uncontrollable laughter. I get ready in record time with the help of Brandy and Megan. While I'm in the shower they put all my stuff in my luggage. Brandy calls down to the front desk to request a cab to the airport and asks for a bellboy to be sent up to help us with our luggage. When we reach the lobby, Brandy gets us checked out of the hotel while Megan and I get our things in the cab. When Brandy finishes at the front desk she climbs in the cab and we're off to the airport. On the ride to the airport all I can think about is Trent. I wonder what happen to him this morning and why he wasn't in the room when I woke. I didn't get to a chance to leave him note thanking him for the most amazing night of my life or to even leave him my contact information. Trent will forever be remembered as the man I had for just one night. I'm drawn out of my though by the questions Brandy and Megan begin asking about last night. Of course we've always shared everything so I tell them every amazing minute from the night before.

Chapter 7

Trent

I've just signed my first contract to choreograph a
new movie that will start production in a few weeks. My
two best buddies, Jackson Harrison and Walter Long, have
joined me at the Skyline bar located on roof of the Nasser
Hotel to celebrate. I've worked really hard to get to this
point and their extremely excited for me. We decide that it
would be safer to rent a room and stay at the hotel since
we'll be drinking. We've been at the bar drinking and
dancing for a couple of hours when I hear Jackson
comment about group of ladies sitting the bar. I turn to see
three beautiful ladies but it's the red head that sparks my
interest. The bartender has sat a shot in front of the red
head and her friends are chanting for her to take the shot.
She smiles, tips her head back and downs the shot like its
water. The sight of this beautiful lady downing that shot is
making me hard. I turn back to Jackson and he leans in to

voice the same comment. He tells me the ladies are getting up and heading to the dance floor. I turn back around just in time to look into a set of amazing hazel eyes. Those eyes are filled with so much passion that I can't turn away. Her eyes have me in a trance and I feel my body tighten with the need to have this woman. One of her friends grabs her hand and pulls her to the dance floor. Love Game, by Lady Gaga is blasting over the speakers and the girls start dancing. They dance in perfect time with each other and I can tell this isn't the first time they've done this.

The crowd moves so the ladies could have more room to dance. I get up from the booth where I've been sitting and make my way to the front of the crowd that has formed around the ladies. Watching the red head move her body to the music makes me even harder. I want to see her ride me with the same amount enthusiasm. When the song changes they change their routine without missing a beat. The longer I watch the red head dance the harder it is to take my eyes off of her. She has long legs and I want to wrap those legs around me and kiss her full lips. They dance to a several more songs before they decide to stop. As soon as they stop she looks directly at me. I've been checking her out while she was dancing. I realize she is now checking me out with the same amount of desire. When she is done checking me out, she looks back into my eyes. I see lust and need in those beautiful eyes. Her eyes are calling me to her so I start walking toward her. When I stop in front of her, I'm a little taller so she has to look up.

"Hi my name is Trent. You're an amazing dancer. Will you dance with me?" I say to her. "Hi my name is Nicole and yes I'd love to dance with you." She replies in a soft whisper. I take Nicole's hand just as Bailando by Enrique Iglesias starts playing. Nicole and I start dancing in perfect rhythm with each other. Our bodies move in sync with one another. I pick Nicole up and she slides back down me. I know she can feel how hard I am. All I want to do is take her back to my room and taste how sweet she is.

When the song finishes I lift and pull her against me, I can feel how hard her nipples are. I can tell she is just as turned on as I am. "Come back to my room with me?" I say in a soft command. I feel her heart rate accelerate and hear a yes whispered back. We start walking to the elevator but she stops us so she can go tell friends she is leaving. She asks me to wait by the elevator for her. I walk over and lean up against the wall to wait for her to return. Nicole is laughing when she breaks through the crowd. That smile of hers is amazing and I can't wait to feel those beautiful lips on me. I see her eyes look me over from head to toe and back up to my eyes. The amount of lust shining back at me from her eyes sends me over the edge. As we step into the elevator, I pick her up and push her against the wall. She wraps her long legs around my waist and it feels great to have her body against mine. Nicole is kissing me like her life depends on our connection. The passion from her kiss is overwhelming my senses. I want to take her here in the elevator but we've reached my floor. I set her down so we can walk to my room.

I can't hold back anymore. I have her against the wall as soon as we walk in the room. Her breast fit perfect in my hands and I massage them through her clothes. I can feel how hard her nipples are as I remove her shirt and bra. I pick her up and she wraps those long sexy legs around me. While still rubbing her right breast I take her left nipple in my mouth. I bite and tug her left nipple with my teeth and then flick it with my tongue. Her soft moans of pleasure push me to move to the right nipple and repeat the same action. Nicole reaches for my shirt. "When I lose a piece of clothing so do you." I smile at her and reply. "That sounds like a terrific idea." I can't take it any longer so I carrier her to the bed. I set her on the edge of the bed. "Nicole I've wanted to taste you ever since I saw you down that shot of whiskey." I start kissing her neck moving down to give her breast more attention. I hear soft moans of pleasure. She's squirming and rubbing against me. I lean back reach for her jeans and she lifts her butt off the bed so I can remove her panties and jeans. I place kisses around her belly button kneel down on my knees to spread her legs wide open. Nicole propped her feet on the side board of the bed. I kiss her left thigh while I use the pad of my thumb to rub her. She releases a loud moan when I put pressure on her nub. "You're so soft and wet." I say as I lick her nub and work my way to her entrance to slide my tongue inside her. Nicole grabs my hair and begins to move her hips in a circle. She tastes so sweet I can't get enough. I lick back to her hard nub and insert two fingers. I continue to push her closer to her orgasm with my fingers and tongue. Nicole starts moving her hips in rhythm with my fingers as they move in and out of her. "Trent I'm about to cum." I hear her moan just as I feel her tighten around my fingers. My fingers are covered with her wetness and I can't wait to taste her again. I remove my fingers to lick and suck her sweetness as she comes down from her sexual bliss. "So sweet." I say in a whisper.

Nicole is trying to get her breathing under control as I slowly move to kiss those soft and plump lips. I'm lying on top of her and as I start to push myself up I help her sit up. I still have my pants on she reaches to unbutton my jeans and slides them off. Nicole leans to lick the moisture off so the head and lick down to the base of my cock. Her sweet lips are going to kill me. They're soft and feel good on my cock. Nicole stands, turns, and pushes me so I'm sitting on the bed. She kneels between my legs. "I want to taste you now." Is all Nicole says as she takes my cock in her mouth with a licking and sucking motion. She grips my cock in her hand and slides up and down in rhythm with her mouth. I release a deep moan of pleasure and begin moving in rhythm with Nicole. Nicole mouth is driving me closer to my orgasm with each suck and lick. She has stopped so I open my eyes to find Nicole looking up at me. She moves to put my cock back in her mouth but I can't wait any longer. I want to slide my cock deep inside her. Before she has a chance to continue, I grab her

around the waist and sit her on my lap. We slide back on
the bed so she can straddle me. The head of my cock is at
her entrance and she slowly moves down my cock. "Nicole
you're so tight. I don't want to hurt you." I whisper in her
ear. "Don't worry the pleasure I feel out weights the pain."
Is her reply. As she slowly slides further down my cock. I
grab the back of her head to pull her in for a deep kiss. As
soon as she has accommodated to my size we start moving
with the same rhythm we've had all night long.

Nicole is sliding up and down my cock. Stopping
just as the head of my cock is about to slide out. She then
slides back down so I can fill her again. I can tell her
orgasm is building because she is moving faster and
harder. With each movement she is driving me closer to my
own orgasm. I need to take control and bury deep inside
her. Nicole leans in to kiss me and I take this chance to flip
us over so I'm on top. I'm pushing in and out of her faster,
harder and burying my cock deep in her. I hear Nicole
moan. "Harder Trent. I want it harder. You won't hurt me
I'm almost there." Nicole telling me what she needs and
wants sends me over the edge. I begin moving faster and
hitting harder. I push in deep one more time we cum at the
same time. We moan with pleasure as we continue to ride
the wave till we have nothing left. Shit this feels damn
good.

Hell, Nicole is amazing; I'm still inside her and can't
think of anything but starting round two. Nicole is the first
woman that I've went to bed with who isn't afraid to say

what she wants and then demand to receive it. I want more and I'm not sure if just one night will be enough to put out the need I have to be inside her. I smile at her and ask. "Are you ready for round two? I can't get enough of your sweet body." Nicole slowly starts moving her hips in a circular motion and my cock is getting harder. Nicole moans her reply. "Yes, let's see who will tire out first." Her response causes me to laugh. I match the movement of her hips with my own pushing motions. As I slowly push deep in her again. I reply with a soft laugh. "Baby I'm up for the challenge." Nicole is squeezing her wet core around my cock and I know we're going to have a long night.

I wake the next morning to the feel of a warm, soft, and naked body next to me. I move and damn my muscles haven't been this sore since I attended my first dance class. The memories from last night play through my mind. I remember everything I did to that body and what Nicole did to mine. We ended with a draw last night. Neither one of us wanted to give up first but by five am our bodies were so exhausted that we passed out. Nicole is on her side with her back to me the sheet is lying just above her breast. I want rub her breast and watch the nipple harden so I can suck on it again. The sun is shining on her from the window and I realize for the first time how nice it would be to have someone to wake up with. Her brown and red highlights are shining in the sunlight. I really hate to move but we both need something to eat so we can have the strength for another round this morning. I slide out of the bed careful not to wake her and get dressed. I grab a piece of hotel stationary to leave a note on the night stand next to her.

Good morning baby. Gone to café to grab us some coffee and something to eat will be back shortly. Trent

The whole way to the café, I remember how amazing it felt to connect with a Nicole. Nicole is fun, demanding, and self-confident enough to tell you what she wants. We have more than a physical connection and I want explore what that connection is. I walk into the café and order our food. While I'm waiting Jackson and Walter come in, they walk over to where I'm standing. "Hi guys. Did you stay out all night?" I ask. "Yes we closed the bar down but had a great time drinking and dancing. So how was your night with the red head?" Walter asks. "Let me just say I've never meet anyone like Nicole before." I reply with a smile. I hear my name called letting me know my order is ready. "I'll catch up with you two later." I tell them as I walk away to pick up the food I'd ordered. As I'm stepping off the elevator on my floor, I faintly hear a door closing but I do not pay any attention to it. I pull the room key from my back pocket and enter the room. I sit the coffee and food on the table so I can wake Nicole. I can tell when I walk into the bedroom that Nicole isn't in the bed so I check the bathroom but she isn't there either. When I exit the bathroom I notice that her things are gone. Damn it she's gone, I check to see if she left a note but I can't find one. I have no way to find her. I only have her first name. I'm filled with a loss that I can't explain. I wanted more than just one night with her and now that isn't going to happen.

Chapter 8

Present day.......Nicole

It's been a few days since I saw Trent no Xzavier. Hell I'm not sure what to even call him. He introduced himself as Trent when I meet him five years ago. I can't really judge him for that since I did the exact same thing by giving him my middle name. I've been running for a while this morning but running hasn't help with the emotions I'm having right now. I was overjoyed to see the man who has haunted my dreams for years but then heartbroken to see him next to his fiancé. Damn it I can't tell if I'm excited, pissed off, or heartbroken. Not having control is driving me crazy. I've stopped running to look out across the ocean when I hear my name. "Sheyenne." I feel the heat from his body as he steps behind me. "Or should I call you Nicole?" I hear the question in his voice. "Nicole is my middle name so you can call by either one." I reply in a low voice. "So

what name should I call you by Xzavier or Trent?" I ask
him in return. "I haven't let another woman call me Trent
since that night you and I spent together. So you can
choose which you want to call me by." He replies. I release
the breath I hadn't realized I was holding. He's standing
behind me so I turn to look at him. His gorgeous blue eyes
still have the same effect on me. I'm lost in a trance and do
not realize he's reached around my waist to pull me closer.
Before I know it he's kissing me and I'm returning the kiss.
The many nights I've thought about having this man's lips
back on me come flooding back. No man after that night
with him has made me feel this excited. A moan escapes
my lips and I pull away. I realize how excited my body has
become. My nipples are hard and my body is humming
with the need to have his lips on me again. A kiss and just
the touch of his body have caused this. I'm pissed with
myself because I have no control. I step a little further back
so I can gain control of my emotions. "Xzavier, why did you
just do that?" I ask. I can't call him Trent, even though
he's the man I spent an amazing night with. This man in
front of me is engaged to be married. He isn't my Trent. "I
wanted to talk with you the other day but you left in a
hurry and I wasn't able to find you." He replied. "I had
other things to take care of and my dad was handling the
rest of the meeting." I reply back. "Do you have a minute
so we can talk?" Xzavier ask with hope in his eyes. I want
to say yes but I'm not sure I can handle being around him
much longer. "Sorry but I've got to get ready for work." I

answer as I turn to leave. "That's fine I'll be here for a few days, so maybe you can have lunch or dinner with me?" He says with a smile. As I look at him I'm taken back to the very first time he smiled at me. "We'll see." I say to him over my shoulder as I walk away.

I run back to the house hoping the run would relieve the ache forming in my chest. I jog up the back porch steps that lead into my bedroom and head straight for the shower to get ready for the day. I close my eyes and let the water run down my face. I still feel his lips on mine and the way his kiss made me feel is driving me crazy. I run my fingers over my lips hoping to wipe the feel of his lips off. The smile he had on his face as he informed me he's going to be here a few days was the same wicked one he used in when we entered the elevator in hotel. He's going to be here for a few days. Oh Hell, I'm not sure I'm going to be able to handle him being here. My body is burning with a desire I haven't had in years. Trent has been the only man that took me over the edge and fulfilled every one of my needs. There have been other men since Trent but none of them have been able to satisfy me the way Trent did. I was hoping Trent would ask me for a place for us to be alone this morning. I was able to feel the ridge of his cock trough his running pants when he pulled me in for the kiss. I know he was just as turned on as I was. I wanted him so bad it hurt. I get out of the shower, walk to my closet, and get dressed. I barely remember fixing my hair and putting my makeup on. Seeing Trent this morning on the beach has me so damn confused that I'm more pissed off than I was this morning.

Chapter 9

Trent

Fate has a sense of humor. You never know when an event will take you by surprise. Seeing Nicole for the first time after five years was wonderful but a total shock. If I hadn't gone with Nikki, I wouldn't have seen Nicole again until the wedding. I could tell she was just as surprised to see me as I was seeing her again but we both hide our shock well. I couldn't show it and she did well hiding it too. It wasn't the time or place for us to talk. I was hoping to get her alone to talk but Nicole had to take a call and left before I could talk with her. Nikki and I left without seeing Nicole again. I haven't been able to get her off my mind since I left the island. I tried to reserve a room as soon as I got back through their website but there weren't any rooms available for the next two months. I continue to drive myself crazy until I finally broke down and called her dad, John Anderson, with the hope he could help me get a room for a week. "Hi Mr. Anderson, its Xzavier Hudson, how are you today? I wanted to see if I could rent one of rooms at the Bed & Breakfast for a week." "Hi Mr. Hudson, all the rooms in the Bed & Breakfast are booked for the next several months but Lilly and I have a few guest rooms in the private living quarters that haven't been used in a while. We would love to have you stay." Mr. Anderson answers back. "Thank you Mr. Anderson. I would be honored to stay in the guest room. Will there be a problem if I came tonight?" I ask. "That's not a problem at all. I'll let housekeeping know so the room will be ready by the time you get here. Also please call me John." Mr. Anderson tells me. "Yes, Sir, please call me Xzavier as well. Thank you again for allowing me to stay in your home." I reply as we end our call. It was late when I got to Bed & Breakfast but John was true to his word. The guest room was ready for me.

This morning I decide to go for a jog on the beautiful beach instead of using the onsite gym. The morning sun and fresh air will do me good. To my knowledge Nicole isn't aware that I'm here or planning to stay for a week. John and Lilly invited me to eat breakfast with them this morning after my morning jog. I've been jogging for a few minutes when I see Nicole standing on the beach looking at the sunrise. The morning sun light is reflecting off her hair as it did the morning after our amazing night. I want to run my hands through her hair and kiss those soft lips. I walk

over to where she is standing so I can finally speak to her.
I'll have to control myself so I don't pull her my arms and
kiss her the way I've wanted to kiss her the last five years.
"Sheyenne or should I call you Nicole?" I ask as I walk up
and stand behind her. "Nicole is my middle name so you
can call me by either one." She replies in a low voice. "So
what name should I call you by Xzavier or Trent?" Nicole
asks me in return. "I haven't let another woman call me
Trent since the night you and I spent together. So you can
choose which you want to call me by." I reply. Nicole turns
around and looks up at me. Her beautiful eyes have me in
a trance and my will power is gone. I've wanted to look into
those beautiful eyes again for so long that it's hard to
believe that she is standing in front of me. I reach out and
pull her close so I can kiss those sexy lips. I'm
automatically taken back to our one night together. She
releases a moan and pulls away. I could feel her nipples
harden as we kissed. "Xzavier, why did you just do that?"
She asks. I've wanted to do that ever since I saw her the
other day. "I wanted to talk with you the other day after the
meeting. You left in a hurry and I wasn't able to find you."
I tell her. "I had other things to take care of and my dad
was handling the rest of the meeting." Nicole replies back.
"Do you have a minute so we can talk?" I ask hoping she'll
say yes. "Sorry but I've got to get ready for work" she
answers as she turns to leave. "That's fine I'll be here for a
few days, so maybe you can have lunch or dinner with me?"

I reply with a smile. "We'll see." Is all she says to me over her shoulder as she walks away.

I'm not sure what's keeping her from talking with me but I'm not a quitter. I could feel her desire in the kiss as she kissed me back.

Chapter 10

Nicole

I'm walking up the steps to the kitchen to have breakfast with my family, as we do every morning; I hear my mom and dad talking with Xzavier. What the hell is he doing in the kitchen with my parents? I stopped on the steps when I hear Xzavier. I was lost in thought and didn't hear Sasha walk up behind me. "What's wrong Shy? Why haven't you gone in?" she asks. I turn to answer her but then she hears Xzavier talking to our parents. She gives me a questioning look. "He is driving me freaking crazy. I saw him on the beach this morning and he kissed me. I'm not sure how much longer I'm going to be able to keep it together. My emotions are so tight that running in the mornings isn't helping. All I can remember is the one night we had together but then I see him standing next to Nikki." I tell her shaking my head. "I'm sorry Shy, I wish there was something I could do to help. Mom and dad are letting him stay in the guest room." She tells me. "Damn it, have they realized who he is?" I ask. "I'm not sure if dad has but I think mom has." She says as she walks past me into the kitchen.

I pull myself together so I can walk in behind Sasha. "Good morning." I say as I walk in the door. I walk over to the coffee pot to fix me a cup of coffee. I hear everyone's replies to my greeting. "Xzavier how was your run this morning on the beach?" I ask. "It was very relaxing. The beach is a beautiful place to run as the sun is rising." He replies between bites of pancakes. "Yes it is. I run every morning that I can." I tell him. I give mom and dad a kiss on the cheek as I sit next to mom to eat. I choose to sit away from Xzavier so I can keep my wits and maybe my emotions in check. Xzavier is sitting across from me and man it is even sexy to watch him eat. I clearly remember how it felt to have those lips on me.

Mom, Dad, and Xzavier continue their conversation and I try to tune them out while I'm getting myself under control. "Xzavier, what do you do for a living?" Xzavier looks up from his plate as he puts the last bite of pancake in his mouth. He leans back in the chair before he answers dad's question. "I own my own dance company. I choreograph dance routines for movies, music videos, and sometimes I've even help with dance routines for concerts. I've been doing this for the last five years." "That's sounds like a lot of fun. Shy is a wonderful dancer, her and her two best friends were the lead dancers for their high school dance line." Mom tells him as she is patting me on the hand. I look up to see the sparkle in Xzavier's eyes. I know he's remembering our dance together. "Lilly, I would love to see Sheyenne dance. Maybe we can even dance together sometime." Xzavier smiles at mom and comments. "Maybe Shy can take some time and show you the dance studio so y'all can dance together." My mom replies back with her beautiful smile. Yep, my mom knows exactly who Xzavier is. Damn it I've got to get out of here. I stand up and take my coffee cup and plate to the dishwasher. I feel Xzavier watching me. "Are you done honey?" My dad asks. "Yes Sir I have several things to work on this morning so I'm heading to my office to get started. Y'all have a wonderful morning." I walk over to mom and dad and give them a kiss good bye.

I leave mom, dad, Sasha, and Xzavier in the kitchen and head to my office to work. I have a meeting this morning with the construction supervisor to review the progress on the additional rooms. The construction is on schedule and as long as the weather stays in our favor the construction will be completed ahead of schedule. During the walk to my office thoughts of Trent fill my head. I won't be able to get anything done if I keep this up. I wave to Ashley as I pass the reception desk. Working is the only way I'm going to stop thinking about him. So I sit at my desk and busy myself with work. Before I know it time has flown by. I hear the meeting reminder ding on my computer. I'm getting up from my desk to leave when Ashley comes over the intercom. "Ms. Anderson, Xzavier Hudson would like to see you." "Thanks Ashley, I'm on my way out to the office now so I'll see what he needs." I reply. As I shut my office door, I see Xzavier standing next to Ashley's desk smiling and joking with her. His beautiful eyes and smile along with his gorgeous face can make any woman stop and take notice.

"Hi Xzavier walk with me, I'm on my way to a meeting." I say as I walk past him. He turns around and falls in step with me. "What can I do for you, Xzavier?" I ask. "For starterss will you please have lunch with me? I would like to talk with you." He replies. "You're not going to leave me alone until I do are you?" I say with a sigh. "No, I'm here for the next seven days so we can do this now or I'll keep asking until you given in." Xzavier replies with a snicker. This causes me to stop and look at him. "Xzavier, what is there talk about? We had a wonderful night together five years ago and now you're engaged to be married in a couple of months." By this time we've made it to the construction site and I see the manager waiting for me. "But, yes I'll have lunch just so you can get it out of your system. Meet me at 12:30 in the restaurant. I've got to go for my meeting." I tell him as I walk way and head toward the supervisor.

The new rooms look amazing and from the progress I see they will be completed at least two weeks ahead of schedule. The first guest we have booked to use the new rooms happens to be the wedding guest for Nikki Clouse's wedding. This though makes me sad. I'll have to talk with Sasha and make sure she has a job that will keep me in the kitchen for the wedding. I won't be able to see Xzavier marry Nikki. I shake off that thought and continue to walk with Jake, the construction supervisor, to the single home we've had built as a Honeymoon cabin. The cabin is located in a secluded area with a private beach. This will give the newlyweds alone time or they can come to the main house and have access to all of our accommodations. I finish talking to Jake and look at my phone to see I still have about forty five minutes before I'm to meet Xzavier for lunch. I really hope this talk is short and sweet and he decides to spend the rest of his time here relaxing. I'll do whatever I can to avoid Xzavier while he's here. I stand on the porch attached to the cabin and look out at the beach to see the ocean waves rolling up and then slowly sliding back down. I start thinking about the kiss Trent and I had this morning and how wonderful it would be to make love to him on the beach with the waves flowing around us. I bring myself out of the daydream and start walking back to the restaurant to have lunch with Xzavier.

I walk up to the hostess station and start to walk to the kitchen when Sue, the lunch hostess stops me. "Good afternoon Ms. Sheyenne. Mr. Hudson is waiting for you in the private dining area." She tells me as I come to a stop in front of her. "Thank you Ms. Sue." I tell her as I walk to the dining room. I open the doors and find Xzavier sitting at one of the booths in the corner. He's talking on his phone but he waves at me when he sees me walk in. As I get closer he ends his call and stands to greet me. "Hi Sheyenne, how did your meeting go this afternoon?" He asks as we sit down. "It was a very productive meeting. The construction is head of schedule and they have finished the Honeymoon cabin. The view of the private beach from the porch is breath taking. You and Nikki are going to enjoy it." I tell him. The thought of them together is breaking my heart. I keep my facial expressions neutral so he can't tell. Xzavier smiles at that statement and so sweetly says to me. "Nicole, I'm not engaged to Nikki, my brother, Jeremiah is." I hear a gasp escape my lips.

Chapter 11

"Nicole, are you okay?" Xzavier ask me when I don't say anything. I have so many thoughts running through my head that I have no idea what to say to him. The waiter happens to come up to take our drink and food order. I order a glass of coke with Sasha's daily special and Xzavier orders the same. Sasha's daily special today is pasta with meat sauce topped with fried green tomatoes. Xzavier waits until the waiter has left before he asks again "Nicole, are you okay? You haven't said a word since I told you I wasn't getting married." All I can do is stare at Xzavier with the hope I'm not dreaming. "I'm trying to process the information. When you walked in the day of the appointment, it felt like my heart had been ripped out of my chest. I've dreamed of seeing you again so many times in the past five years. Then out of nowhere you just happen to walk in my dad's office with a client to talk to about her wedding. I thought I would die right there." I manage to say. "Nicole believe me I was just as caught off guard as you were. I've thought about you a lot over the past five years. My brother wasn't able to get away from work so he asked if I would accompany Nikki and I was more than happy to help. I didn't realize you thought I was her fiancé until the end of the meeting when you told us we were going to be very happy. I tried to find you but you weren't anywhere to be found. I couldn't stay that day because of my schedule but when I got back I couldn't work for thinking about you. Your parents were kind enough to allow me to use the guest bedroom in the private living quarters, since all the rooms were booked." He tells me as he's getting up out of his seat. Xzavier comes to my side of the booth and slides in next to me.

"Hi, my name is Xzavier Trent Hudson." He says with a devilish smile. "Hello Trent, my name is Sheyenne Nicole Anderson; it's a pleasure to meet you." I say with a smile. "Now that we've gotten that out of the way, I can do this." He says as he is leans in and kisses me. I lean into the kiss and kiss him back with all the passion and need I have for him. We both break away when we hear a soft cough. We look up at the same time to see Sasha standing there looking at us. "Okay I guess you know he isn't engaged." Sasha says to me. Sasha has our meal and she sets the plates down on the table. Xzavier moves back to his side of the booth as Sasha pulls up a chair to take a seat at the end of the table. "Wait you knew he wasn't engaged to Nikki and you haven't told me." I said to Sasha when her statement finally registered. "In her defense, she only found out this morning. After you left at breakfast, your parents, Sasha, and I were talking and it came up about the wedding. You're mom asked how long Nikki and I have been engaged. I informed them that my brother was her fiancé not me. I was going to tell you this morning on the beach but you didn't give me a chance to." Xzavier explained. I nod my head at his explanation. "Well I've got to get back to the kitchen. Enjoy your lunch." Sasha says as she gets up to leave. "See you later Sash, we have a conference call with Nikki's wedding planner today at three." I remind her as she starts walking away. "See ya then." She yells over her shoulder as she enters the kitchen.

Xzavier and I start eating our meals. "This is amazing. Sasha is a terrific chef." Xzavier says as he puts another bite in his mouth. "Yes she is. She tours around the world to find new dishes to serve here at the restaurant. Sasha just returned from Italy." I tell him. "You must be very proud of her." He states. "We are very proud of her. Sasha has worked hard to be the best Chef she can be." I say through a smile. "You have a beautiful smile, Nicole. I've remembered that smile every day for the past five years. The first time I saw you smile was at the bar right before you took that shot. I knew then that you were something special." Trent tells me. "Thank you. Your eyes sparkle more when you smile. I knew from the moment I looked into your eyes I was in trouble." I tell him as I move my plate. "So Trent, were do we go from here?" I ask.

"I have several ideas but first I would like to get to know you? Even though I remember every inch of your magnificent body, I want to get to know the real Nicole that goes with that wonderful body." He says as he leans over the table to give me a peck on the lips. "So my dear what are your plans for dinner tonight?" Trent asks just as the waiter comes to remove our dishes. "I normally go home and get ready for the next day. Even though tomorrow is Saturday, I review the schedules and make sure we have enough employees scheduled to work. What do you have in mind?" I ask him. "Will you take a walk with me on the beach at sunset?" He asks with a sexy smile that has me squirming in my seat. "Yeah sure I'll be happy to and I have a wonderful place for us to walk. I'll meet you at seven in the kitchen. Thank you for a wonderful lunch. I've got to get back to my office. There are several things on my calendar for this afternoon." I tell him. He helps me out of the booth and kisses me with those soft amazing lips. "Until later." He says between kisses.

As Trent and I are walking out of the dining area, Megan is walking in. The look on her face when she realizes who is standing next to me has me smiling. We walk over to where Megan is standing. "Hi Meg, I see you remember Xzavier or Trent, since that was the name he gave me when we first met." I say once we're standing next to her. Megan takes Xzavier's out reached hand and shakes it. "Yes, I remember him." She says and gives me a questionable look. I haven't taken the time to visit with her since the first day I saw Trent. "Trent this is one of my dearest friends, Megan Jones." I tell Trent as he reaches out to shake Megan's hand. "It's a pleasure to meet you Megan." Trent tells her as he lets go of her hand. Trent leans over and kisses me on the cheek as he tells me. "I'll see you at seven tonight. Megan, again it was a pleasure to meet you." He says as he walks by.

"Okay chic, why haven't you told me about meeting sex on a stick again?" she asks. "Megan, it was such a shock. I thought he was engaged to our new client." I tell her. Megan picks up her lunch and we start walking back to her office. I explain everything to her on the walk back to her office. She's shaking her head when I'm done. "That's just crazy, Shy. After five years he walks back into your life. So what's happening now?" She asks. "Well, he wants to get to know each other and I really like that idea. Just being around him makes me feel good. It's like we haven't been apart for five years. I know we only spent one night together and that night was spent taking care of a physical need we had. For some reason, I feel that we have more than that physical connection and that we are meant to be together. Call me crazy but I fell in love with him five years ago." I tell her with a smile and a sigh. "So are you going to tell him?" She asks me. "Yeah, I plan to but not right now. That would be a lot to lay on someone you've just meet officially for the first time." I reply. "Shy let me know if you need me and I'll be there." Megan replies as she walks into her office. "I know I can count on you. See you later." I say as I turn to walk back to my office.

I still have about an hour and half before the scheduled conference call with Nikki Clouse's wedding planner, Liv Kross. So I head back to my office to work on outstanding invoices, place orders, and review the online reservations. Since starting as manager I've been able to automate several of the accounting procedures that mom supervises. This allows me to have more time to manage the Bed & Breakfast. Sasha knocks on my office door, just as I'm finishing up with my afternoon task. "Come in Sasha, we have a few minutes before the conference call." I tell her as she sits in the next to me. "How was lunch today?" She asks with a smile. "The meal was fantastic. I'll have to let the chef know she out did herself again." I answer her with a laugh. I know what she is really asking but I decide to aggravate her a little bit. "I bet the chef would love to hear that but you know what I'm really asking about." She replies while giving me a look saying don't even try to get out of telling her what she wants to know. I'm saved from having to give her any information when Ashley calls over the intercom. "Ms. Anderson, there is a Ms. Liv Kross on the phone." "Thanks Ashley, we're ready so please transfer the call." I reply. I hear Ashley reply "Yes ma'am." As she is transfers the call.

"Hi Ms. Kross, I'm Sheyenne Anderson and my sister Sasha Anderson is also on the call today." I tell her once I know the call has been transferred. "Thank you, please call me Liv and is it okay for me to call you by Sasha and Sheyenne?" Liv asks. "Yes ma'am that would be terrific." Sasha replies. "Okay ladies. Nikki has told me all about the beautiful location for the wedding and reception. I can't wait to see the location in person. I was hoping we could schedule a time next week for me to come down for the day. We only have six weeks to make sure everything is in order for the big day." Liv is all business when she starts talking. "We would love to have you." I tell her. "Now it's my understanding that there are to be about a hundred guests attending the wedding but not all will be staying the night here at the Bed & Breakfast. The construction on the new rooms is ahead of schedule and should be completed in the next two weeks. The honeymoon cabin is complete and the view of the private beach is breath taking." I inform Liv. "That is really good to hear. Also, Sasha the menu for the reception is to die for. I can't wait to try the items on the menu." She informs Sasha. "I'm pleased you love the menu." Sasha replies. As Liv and Sasha are talking I pull up our calendar to find a day nest week for Liv to visit. "Liv is Wednesday, June 16 good for you. That would be next week." I ask. "Yes that day would fit perfectly in my schedule." She replies. "Great we look forward to seeing you then. We can draw out more definite plans that day. Thank you for giving us a call today Liv hope you have a wonderful evening." I tell her. "Thank you ladies and hope you do too." She says, as she's hanging up the phone.

"Sash, what did Nikki decide to have on the menu?" I ask. "The guest will have small grilled steaks, lobster tail, pasta, a salad, and grilled vegetables. For dessert she wants red velvet cupcakes, individual peach cobbler cups, and small individual strawberry cheesecakes." She replies. "Wow that is a great menu. So will you make all the desserts or will you order those?" I ask. "Actually I have someone else in mind to help out with the desserts. He and I went to a culinary class together. Lee was really great with the desserts." She tells me but I can tell that her thoughts are elsewhere. I think there is a story here but I choose to leave it alone for now. Sasha snaps out of her thoughts and looks over at me. "So are you going to tell me how lunch went today?" She asks. "I was hoping you had forgotten. Lunch went very well. Xzavier wants to get to know each other. We're going for a walk on the beach at sunset." I say with a smile. I check my watch and notice it's almost 4:00 o'clock and I have nothing else on my schedule. "Sash, I think I'm going to call it a day. Are you going back to the kitchen?" I ask as I get up from my desk. "Yeah, I've got to go back and make sure everything is ready for supper and the work schedule is filled to cover room service calls." She says as she is getting up and walking toward the door. "Have a good evening Shy. Hope you have a great walk with Xzavier." She tells me from the doorway before she walks out. "Thanks and you too." I tell her. I still have a few hours before my walk with Trent. I decide to go home, change into comfortable clothes and unwind from my emotional day.

Chapter 12

When I get home I decided to work off some of the stress from today. I change into my favorite black yoga pants, a yellow sports bra and white tank top. A good work out will help me relax before my walk with Trent. I gather my things and head over to the gym. The dance studio happens to be on the way to the gym so I glance in to see if anyone is in there. To my surprise I see Trent dancing and my goodness he is sexy. His body is moving in such a sexual rhythm that I'm getting turned on just watching him. It's at that moment that I realize why I've been on such an emotional roller-coaster. From the moment I saw him for the first time again, my body has been craving his touch. No man since Trent has been able to make my body burn with a need so deep that it's became consuming. I've tried to find someone else that could make me feel the way he did but no one can. I've been told there is one person in this world for you. This person will help complete you in

every way. Trent and I connected on more than a physical
level five years ago. I hope fate isn't playing a cruel joke by
bringing him back just to take him from me again. Before I
realize what I'm doing, I've open the door and walked into
the dance studio. Trent is so in tune with the music and
dance he's doing that he hasn't noticed I've entered the
room. He continues to move his body with the rhythm of
the beat. By the time the song ends I'm standing behind
him. Trent turns and is surprised to see me standing there.
"Hi Nicole, sorry I tune everything out when I'm dancing
and didn't hear you come in." He says with a sexy smile.
He takes a step closer so now our bodies are inches from
touching. "It's okay; I didn't want to disturb you. I enjoyed
watching you dance." I say back as I step closer so now our
chests are touching. I'm so twisted with desire that I can't
think of anything else but getting his body next to mine.
"Dance with me again?" Trent asks as he's taking my
hand. "Yes." Comes out as a whisper. Trent pulls me into
his arms and we begin to move and sway to the beat of the
music. Our bodies are so in sync that we move in a perfect
rhythm. It's like we've danced together our whole lives.
The longer we dance the harder he becomes. I can feel his
hard ridge rubbing up against me. My body is responding
to his excitement. I'm sure he can feel the hardness of my
nipples as they rub against him. I've got to get him inside
me soon or I'm going to combust from the fire burning
inside. Trent blue eyes are filled with the lust that I feel. I
know he must be thinking the same thing.

Trent picks me up and I lock my legs around his waist. I bend to whisper in his ear. "Trent, I need you now! I want to feel you inside me." I manage to say between moans. "Baby, I thought you would never ask. Where can we go? I'm not sure the studio is the best place." He whispers back as he sucks on my earlobe. That single action causes me to release a loud moan and move my hips in circular motion. "We'll be okay. Walk me over to the door and the windows." I ask him. Trent carries me over to them and I close the blinds, lock the door, and make sure the closed sign is posted. Trent pushes me up against the wall next to the door and pushes his hard ridge against my already throbbing core. I lean in and kiss him softly at first but the longer we're touching the more passionate the kiss becomes. "Set me down so I can take my pants off." I request. Trent smiles and sets me down. "When you lose a piece of clothing so do I." He says as he pulls his shirt over his head. Trent remembers the line I told him five years ago. This makes me smile. I get a good look at his well defined chest and his six pack abs. Trent was muscular five years ago but now his muscles are more defined. The many hours of dancing has sculpted a well defined set of abs. Oh holy hell that V at his hips is driving me crazy. As I'm looking over his gorgeous body I notice a tattoo that wasn't there five years ago. He sees me looking at the tattoo that runs just under his first rib. "I got it a few weeks after our night together." He tells me. I lean in closer to read the tattoo. "*Mine for Just One Night*" I run my fingers along the words as I read the tattoo out loud and turn to look him in the eyes. I see the passion I feel reflecting back in his eyes.

I step up closer so our chest are touching and stand on my tip toes so I can kiss him. "Pick me up and walk over to the ballet bar." I tell him. I still have my tank top on but I remove my sports bra as he carries me over to the bar. Trent takes one hand and slides it between us so he can rub my already sensitive nub. He then slides his fingers to my wet entrance. "Nicole you are so wet." He says as he slides two fingers in me. I release a soft moan at the pleasure I feel from this simple touch. We've made it to the ballet bar so he balances me on the bar while he pulls his pants down to his knees. Trent takes me off the bar, positions me around his waist so I can slide down his extremely hard cock. I feel the head at my entrance and he slowly pushes inside. The feeling makes both of us grown in pleasure. I take my arms and hands and place them on the bar so I can support myself. At this angle Trent can push deeper inside me and damn does it feel good. "Damn Nicole you feel so good." Trent says between pushes. I use the bar for support so I can start moving with Trent. The feel of him sliding in and out of me is sending both of us closer to our orgasm. Moans of pleasure are steadily coming out of me. "Oh you feel so good. Please a little harder. I'm almost there. Faster Trent." I feel my release getting closer and closer with each push. I'm glad this studio is sound proof or anyone walking by would be able to hear us. "Nicole, I'm almost there. Cum with me." Trent says as he slams into me harder and harder. His words send me over the edge and I cum extremely fast and hard. I feel Trent find his release at the same time I do. When we both slowly stop moving, Trent steps closer to the bar so I can wrap my arms around his neck and we lean together for a soft passionate kiss.

Trent breaks the kiss and asks. "Where is the bathroom? We need to get cleaned up before we leave." I point in the direction of the bathroom and say. "Just through those doors." Trent's pants have completely fallen to the floor. He steps out of them so he can carry me to bathroom. The whole time he is still inside me. The walking motion is causing him to rub me and I can feel the making of another orgasm. The motion is causing his cock to grow longer and thicker. I lean in and whisper in his ear. "I think we're ready for round two." I lean back so I can see his face. He chuckles and replies. "Let's see who can tires out first? But if I remember last time it was a draw." "Yes, I hate to lose." I sweetly reply. We've made it to the bathrooms and I lead him to the private bathroom that family uses. Trent opens the door and closes it behind us before he heads to the sink. He sets me on the counter and then kneels between my legs. "I've wanted to taste you since our kiss this morning." He tells me before he takes my legs and places them over his shoulders. Before I know it he has slid my ass to the edge and begins licking me. His fingers are teasing my nub. He slides his tongue in me and I start following the motion he begins. He licks from my entrance to my nub and begins to suck on it while sliding two fingers in and out of me. "Trent baby I feel another orgasm building. You feel so good. Don't stop. Yes! Right there that's the spot." I manage to say between moans. "Come on baby give it to me. I want to taste you." Trent says as he takes his fingers and spreads me wider. He's sucking, licking, and blowing on me, which pushes me into the sweetest orgasm. The high from it feels unbelievable. Trent is acting like it's the sweetest dessert he's ever had. Trent finishes licking up the last of my orgasm, removes my legs from his shoulders, and slides me back from the edge of the counter. Trent reaches over to the linen shelf and grabs a wash cloth. I watch him as he turns on the water in the sink and he checks to water temperature to make sure it's okay before he wets the wash cloth. Trent takes his time cleaning me, making sure I'm wiped completely clean. Once I'm clean enough by his standards, he rinsed the wash cloth and cleans himself. He throws the wash cloth in the dirty hamper and turns back to me with a smile on his face. Trent grabs me around the waist and helps me down. He takes my hand in his and leads me back into the studio.

Our clothes are all over the studio. Trent walks past me and I get an eye full of his sexy ass and his lean back. Trent is built and now I know why it wasn't any trouble for him to have sex while standing and supporting me at the same time. I can't wait to see what else his body can handle. I look up to see Trent smiling at me. He has caught me checking out his body. "You keep looking at me like I'm a piece of meat you can eat and we'll never make it out of this studio." He tells me as he's bending down to pick up his pants. "I still owe you one for the bathroom. So later I'll get to have a taste of you." I say to him as I walk by to retrieve my pants from near the door. Before I can make it past him, he grabs my arm and pulls me in for a kiss. I feel his cock harden so I drop to my knees and take his cock my mouth and begin to suck. The harder I suck the harder he becomes. I lick around the head and down to the base and back up. I wrap my hands around the bottom and start moving up as I'm moving down with my mouth. "Nicole your mouth feels so good." Trent growls out. He starts moving with my rhythm and I hear him moan in pleasure. I pull my lips over my teeth and rub harder. "Holy shit, you're driving me crazy." Trent says right as he starts to cum. I make sure that I've licked him clean and I stand. "Now we're even." I say as I walk over to where my pants are so I can put them on. "You're going to be the death of me." Trent tells me when he stops to stand beside me and retrieves his shirt from the floor. "But think of the fun we'll have in the process." I laugh and say.

"Do you want to grab supper before we go for our walk?" I ask him. "Yes, that would be great. Let's meet in the kitchen after we've both gotten cleaned up from this afternoon's workout." He replies back. "Sounds like a plan to me. See you in thirty. I unlock the door so we can leave. Trent pulls me in for a quick kiss before we head in different directions. I walk out the door a few seconds behind Trent and turn to see my mom standing at the end of the hallway. Mom sees me as I come out of the room and gives me a big smile. I start walking toward her. "How are you doing this afternoon mom?" I ask when I get close enough she can hear me. "I'm fine sweetheart. How are you?" She asks back. "I'm good mom." I say when I come to a stop next to her. "So I see you two took my suggestion about dancing." She snickers and shakes her head. "I take it that Xzavier is Trent you meet five years ago." She asks. "Yes, ma'am you're correct. We're going to have supper and take a walk afterwards." I tell her. "Well, I hope y'all have a wonderful time. Y'all have a lot to talk about. Five years is a long time and a lot can happen. I really hope everything works out." Mom says as she kisses me on the check. "Thanks mom, I hope it does to. Have a wonderful night. Love ya." I say as I start to walk past her. "Love you too sweetheart." I hear her say back.

I make it home and take a quick shower. Since it's still nice out and not to overly hot and humid, I decide to wear blue jean cut off shorts with a fitted pale pink tank top. My favorite pink and white flip flops will be perfect for a walk on the beach. I've toweled dried my hair and pull it up into a ponytail. I glance over to the clock on the night stand and realize thirty minutes has flown by. Instead of walking all the way through the house, I decide to use the door in my bedroom to leads out to the wraparound porch.

The walk to the private kitchen doesn't take long. As I'm entering from the doorway, Trent is walking in from the hall that leads to the private living quarters. "Hi Trent, would you like to go and eat in the restaurant or we can find something in here to eat." I ask once we've both made it to the breakfast bar. "Here will be fine with me. So what do you want?" He asks in return. "I think I'll make a salad." I say as I'm walking to the fridge to grab the supplies to make my salad. "Do you want a salad or a sandwich? We have a lot of sandwich meat and if you can't find it in this fridge we can go to the main kitchen." I tell him as I turn to set the supplies on the corner. "A sandwich would be great." He tells me now that he has walked over to the fridge to grab what he needs. I start adding lettuce, tomato, carrots, eggs, ham, turkey, homemade bacon bits, fried onions, cranberries, pecans, and shredded cheese to the plate in front of me. I glance over to see Trent has stacked his sandwich with roast beef, lettuce, tomato, onions, and mozzarella cheese. Now he's spreading mayo on the fresh hoagie bread made this morning. I take my plate, the vinegar and oil salad dressing, and walk to the other side of the breakfast bar so I can sit down. Trent has finished his sandwich and sits in the seat next to me. I notice neither one of us have taken the time to get something to drink. 'Trent would you like a glass of sweet tea, water, or we also have soda?" I ask as I stand to make myself a glass of sweet tea. "I would love a glass of sweet tea. The glass I had at breakfast was terrific. I typically don't drink sweet tea." I chuckle at his response while I fix both of us a glass of tea. "Yeah that is one thing I remember from my short time in New York. The sweet tea was awful." I tell him as I sit our glasses down next to our plates. Trent laughs along with me. "So what brought you to New York five years ago?" Trent asks just before he takes a bite of his sandwich. "Megan, who you meet earlier in the restaurant, was getting married so Brandy and I planned a girls retreat as a way to celebrate. Brandy is my other best friend. Brandy Holmes, Megan, and I have been friends since grade school. After high school I went to business school, Megan trained to be a Massage Therapist and Brandy went to nursing school. Brandy works in Madison for a Pediatric Endocrinologist and Megan works here at the Bed & Breakfast in the Spa." I explain while I'm pouring the dressing over my salad. "So why were you at the Nasser Hotel that night?" I ask. "Well, I had just signed my first contract and I was celebrating with my two best friends Jackson Harrison and Walter Long. I thought it would be best if we just rented a room at the hotel since we would be drinking." He replies between bites. "That was a very responsible thing to do. We had already been to two other night clubs before we ended up at The Skyline. We were staying at the Nasser as well." I tell Trent. "So how did you like New York?" Trent asks as he is finishing his sandwich and glass of tea. "It was definitely different than any place I've visited before. Which at that time there were very few places I had visited outside of South Carolina. Everything is fast paced and there are so many people. We really enjoyed ourselves though. I've been back several times since then and I enjoy myself each time." I say as I'm getting up from the table. I reach for his empty plate and he stops me. "I can get this." He states as he grabs my plate and empty tea glass. "Trent you're a guest here and it's not your place to clean up the dishes." I tell him as I'm trying to get the dishes back. Trent leans over and whispers in my ear "I think the things we did in the dance studio makes me more than a guest. Oh by the way I can't wait til we can dance again." I sigh deeply at that comment and look at him. Trent has that sexy as hell grin plastered on his face. Man I want to lean over and kiss those sexy lips. His blue eyes are shining with lust. Just as I'm leaning in to kiss him, I hear a soft cough come from behind us. We both lean back and turn to see Jasper standing at the door. Jasper has been an on and off boyfriend for the past four years. He has asked me to marry him about a year ago but I just couldn't say yes. I care about Jasper but it's nothing compared to how I feel for Trent.

"Hi Jasper, how are you tonight?" I ask. Trent has gotten up to put our dishes in the dishwasher. Jasper has walked all the way into the kitchen and now he's standing beside me. He bends downs kisses me on the cheek and looks back at Trent. "I'm doing great. It's a nice evening and I wanted to see if you were up for a walk. It's been a while since we've been able to walk on the beach together." He asks as he turns to look back at me. I look up to see Trent watching us and he doesn't look happy that Jasper is standing so close with his hands on my shoulders. As quick as the look was on Trent's face it's now gone. Trent walks back to his seat next to me. "Where are my manners? Jasper this is Xzavier Hudson. Xzavier this is Jasper Grant." Both men shake hands but you can tell they are sizing each other up trying to figure out who is the better man. Jasper is the same height as Xzavier and they're both muscular. Jasper's shoulders are slightly broader and his muscles are a bigger from the manual labor Jasper's job requires. My body recalls how it feels to have his muscles on me. Hell he is excellent in bed but I can't get past the feeling that I'm not complete when I'm with Jasper. I turn so I can look up at Jasper and I notice the sun has lightened his brown hair. Jasper owns his own construction company. He rebuilds residential homes in disaster areas and new construction homes. "I'm sorry Jasper, I already have plans. Wish I had known you were coming." I can see the disappointment as it flashes across his face when I reply. "Okay that's fine. I just wanted to see you before I left tomorrow. The crew is leaving for Mississippi in the morning. We'll be gone for about two months." He tells me right before he kisses me on the cheek again. Jasper turns and tells Xzavier that it was nice to meet him. "Be careful Jasper and hope y'all stay safe traveling and on the jobsite." I say to him as I stand to give him a hug. He wraps his arms me and squeezes closer to him. He kisses me on the lips this time before he leaves. "Bye Shy. Take care of yourself while I'm gone." He says just before he walks out the door.

"That was interesting." Trent says as I sit back down. "I'd have to agree with you." I say with a sigh. "I take it you two have a history together." Trent asks. "Yeah we do." Was my only reply. I think Trent wants more of an explanation but this is all he is getting right now. I'm a little wound tight from the feel of Jasper's body on mine. Our relationship maybe missing something but our sex life wasn't. "Are you ready for the walk or do you want to wait a little bit?" I ask as a way to change the subject. "I need to make a call before the walk. Can you give me fifteen minutes?" He asks. "Yeah, that's fine. I'll meet you at the beach next to the small boat dock. Do you know where that is?" I reply. "Yes I know where that is see you there." Trent is saying as he's walking back to the private living area.

Chapter 13

Trent

I didn't have to make a phone call. I just needed a few minutes to collect myself. Seeing Nicole and Jasper that close and then he kissed her almost sent me over the edge. It was taking all the strength I had not to do something stupid and then she evades my question about their history. That was the last straw but I have no right to be this upset and possessive. It's not like Nicole and I are in are relationship. We've only slept together twice in five years. Okay breath and let it go. Jasper's is gone and I need to get to the beach so Nicole and I can go for a walk. I leave my room and head for the beach. As I'm walking the trail from the house to the beach, I hear the birds singing and the grasshoppers chirping. The closer to the beach I get I can hear the waves hitting the sand. This is a very relaxing place. I can see why this Bed & Breakfast is doing so well this place is amazing. As I'm exiting the trail I look up to see Nicole standing on the beach barefooted with her back to me. Oh for the love of God, what am I doing? I'm leaving her in six days and I'm not sure if I'll be able to survive when I do. I knew I had feelings for Nicole five years ago but my reaction to Jasper confirmed those feelings are still valid. I've never been that possessive over a woman. I'll have to figure this out before I leave. I quietly walk up behind Nicole wrap my arms around her waist and place a kiss on her cheek. "Hi beautiful, the site of you standing here looking out over the ocean is breath taking." I tell her. She leans into me and with a sigh says. "Thank you Trent." I've noticed she only calls me Trent when we're by ourselves. I wonder why that is. I'll have to ask her why later. I could stand here and hold her like this all night. We fit perfectly together. "Do you want to go for a walk or we could stand here for a while longer. I'm really enjoying holding you." I can tell she is already turned on but I'm not sure if it is because of me or a reaction to Jasper. This pisses me off again. I don't want her to want anyone else when she is with me. Her body should only crave for my touch not a touch of another man. "We can walk now. The sun is setting and the sky is beautiful this time of day. Since you live in New York, this will be a treat for you." She replies as she steps out of my embrace and starts to walk down the beach. I catch up and walk in step with her down the beach. I could care less about the sunset; it's her that I want to spend my time with.

Nicole

Trent walks down the hallway to his room as I leave the kitchen and head down to the beach. It was great to see Jasper. Jasper has been here for me when I needed someone. I do have feelings for him but those feelings do not equal the ones I have for Trent. I was turned on by the kiss he gave me even though I knew what he was trying to do. Trent makes me feel complete like the missing piece of my soul has finally been found. The thing is Jasper is more real than Trent. Trent has been this person from a dream and even though he is here now he's leaving in a few days. I reach the beach and stare at the waves rolling across the ocean to the shore. The sounds and movements of the ocean are soothing and they help me relax. Trent is so good at hiding his feelings I couldn't tell if my interaction with Jasper bothered him. At first I thought I saw something but it was gone so quick that I'm not sure I did.

I'm so focused on the ocean that I didn't hear Trent walk up behind me. He wraps his arms around my waist and kisses me on the cheek. "Hi beautiful, the site of you standing her looking out over the ocean is breathtaking." He tells me. I lean into him and with a sigh I say. "Thank you Trent." "Do you want to go for a walk or we could stand here for a while longer. I'm really enjoying holding you." He asks me. I can tell something is bothering him but I'm not sure what it could be. "We can walk now. The sun is setting and the sky is beautiful this time of day.

Since you live in New York, this will be a treat for you." I reply as I step out of his embrace. I start walking down the beach. Trent catches up and walks in step with me down the beach. We've been walking in silence for the past few minutes as we look out at the ocean. I notice two dolphins playing off in the distance. "Trent, do you see the dolphins playing over there?" I point and ask him. "They look like they're having fun. The sky is a beautiful shade of pink." He replies. "Yeah this isn't something you get to see in New York. Once the sky gets a little darker you will be able to see the stars." I tell him. Trent chuckles. "You have a point. This is definitely something you can't see in New York." The tide is rolling in so the waves are now reaching where Trent and I are walking. The warm water feels great to my bare feet. Trent stops so he can pull his sandals off. He beats the sand off of them and slides one in each back pocket like I've done.

I stopped and turn to face him while he's beating the sand off the sandals. Trent is staring at me like he wants to ask me something but is hesitating. As if he isn't sure he wants to ask the question. "Nicole, what is the deal with you and Jasper?" He finally decides to ask. "Jasper and I have had an on and off relationship for the past four years. He asked me to marry him about a year ago but I wasn't ready so I said no. We still go out when he's home." I explain to him. "Well that explains why he felt the need to kiss you in front of me." Trent replies. There's a flash of emotion on Trent's face but like earlier it's gone before I can realize it. I walk closer to Trent and place my hand on the side of his face. "Trent, I'm no one's property. I knew what Jasper was doing when he kissed me. Not sure why he felt the need to do that. I guess him seeing us so close didn't sit well with him. I do understand that men feel the need to protect what they consider theirs." I say to him as I drop my hand and turn to continue walking down the beach. Trent turns and starts walking with me again. "Trent where did you go the morning after we slept together?" I ask him. I've been waiting five years to find out the answer. Trent grabs my hand to stop me from walking and turns me to face him. He reaches in his back pocket for his wallet and pulls out this folded piece of warn paper. "Nicole, I left to grab us something to eat and drink. I knew we both needed something to replenish our bodies after our long night. I left a note on the night stand on your side of the bed." Trent replies as he's opening the folded paper. Trent finishes opening it and hands it to me. It's the note he wrote on Nasser Hotel stationary.

"Good morning baby. Gone to café to grab us some coffee and something to eat will be back shortly. Trent" I read the note out loud. I look up from reading the worn note with tears in my eyes. He has kept this note for five years. "Trent I didn't see the note. When I woke up and saw the time, I realized I was going to be late for my flight back home if I didn't hurry back to my room. I jumped up got dressed and took the stairs back to my floor. I was kicking myself on the ride to the airport because I didn't leave you a note." I tell him. "When I was stepping off the elevator with our food, I thought I heard a door close. I just thought it was someone entering their room but it could have been the door to the stairwell. I had no way to even try to locate you. We'd only given each other our first names." He says as he's pulling me closer. Before I know it Trent has wrapped one arm around my waist and his other hand is in my hair. Trent starts kissing me softly on the lips. His slow and soft kisses are amazing. I've lifted my arms and place them around his neck so I can lean into him more. His kisses are turning me on and I can tell Trent is turned on too. "Nicole, you have filled my dreams for so long that I began to think I dreamed our night together. To be able to hold you again has been beyond amazing. One night with you wasn't enough." Trent tells me after he stops kissing me. I'm so turned on. "Trent, you have also lived in my dreams and when you walked in my dad's office I almost didn't believe it was you." I tell Trent when I lean back to look him in the eyes. The sun has completely set and the moon has begun to rise in the sky. Trent and I are surrounded by the glow from the full moon. I want Trent so bad that I'm aching for his touch but I know we need to slow down. He's only here for a short time and then he'll be gone again. "Let's finish this walk so I can show you more of this beautiful island." I tell him as I step out of his embrace. Trent grabs my hand and doesn't let go of it. We finish walking around the island. I'm pointing out the different stars and how the waves look at night. Trent is taking everything in and seems to be enjoying our walk. We've made it back to my house and we're standing on my front porch. "Nicole, I've enjoyed spending the afternoon with you. Can we spend more time together tomorrow?" Trent asks. "Yes, I would love to spend the day with you. I've got to get up in the morning and work for a few hours but have the rest of the day off. When I get done I'll come by and get you." I tell him. "Sure that's fine with me. Goodnight Nicole." Trent says as he steps closer to give me a kiss. I so want to ask him in to spend the night in bed together but I know that's not the best thing to do right now. "Goodnight Trent, see you in the morning." I say as I turn to walk in the house.

Chapter 14

I lean up against the door once I've shut it. It was difficult to keep myself from inviting Trent in. I could've finally allowed my dreams to come true. I want to spend more time with him but I can't allow myself the luxury. I have too many things to consider when it comes to Trent. I walk to my bedroom and decide to take another shower and relax. After my shower, I sit down at my desk and work on my Things To Do list for Nikki Clouse's wedding. This will be one of the biggest events we've held at the Bed & Breakfast so everything has to go as planned. Working will help me keep my mind off the fact that Trent isn't that away from me.

Nikki Clouse's wedding - August 2, 2014

  o *Guest total*

    ▪ *Attending wedding – 125*

    ▪ *Staying @ B&B – 80-90*

- *Supplies to check on*
  - *Tables*
  - *Chairs*
  - *Tents (in case of rain)*
  - *Portable cots for extra bedding if needed.*
  - *Extension cords*
- *Talk with Sasha to see what extra items she needs*
- *Hire part time staff for event – talk with Ashley*
- *Meeting with Liv Kross*
  - *Have an understanding of the requirements Bed & Breakfast will have vs what Liv's company will handle*
  - *Work out plan for ceremony and reception*
- ***Start interview process to staff the new additions. Talk with Ashley on Monday.*

I look up from my notes and realize it's almost eleven thirty. I think this is a good start. I know there will be a lot to do between now and the wedding. I get up from the desk and climb in bed. Work was a great distraction but now that I'm trying to sleep all I can think about is Trent's soft kisses. This is going to be a long night. Just thinking about him is turning me on. It was much easier when he only lived in my dreams.

Trent

I haven't had a sleepless night like last night in a very long time. I was thinking Nicole was going to invite me in last night. I could tell she was just as turned on as I was. I can't figure out why she didn't invite me in. Maybe it had something to do with seeing Jasper. They seemed to have feelings for each other when they were together last night. Jasper isn't the right person for Nicole, I am. I want her in my life but I'm not sure how to do that. When I got back to my room last night I had to work so I wouldn't drive myself insane thinking about Nicole. I have to leave on Thursday so I can make a meeting with a new client Friday morning. I scheduled my flight back to New York and sent an email with my itinerary to my personal assistant, Anna. I've asked Anna to make sure all the paperwork is ready for the new client and confirm the meeting time. I was able to review a renewal contract for a current client and send the revisions to Anna. Anna has been with me for the last three years. Three years ago when it finally got to the point where I couldn't keep up with the business and dancing side of the company I decided hiring a personal assistant was the best course of action. Anna has been a great addition.

I've been up for a few hours just lying here in the bed thinking of Nicole. I need to get up and get ready to spend another terrific day with Nicole. I take a quick shower and get dressed. Maybe Nicole is already in the kitchen having breakfast and I can see what she has planned for today. I shut the door to my room and start walking up the hallway towards the kitchen. When I get about halfway to the kitchen I can hear Nicole talking with her dad. "No dad I've got this under control. There's nothing to worry about. Please let me handle this in my own way." I hear Nicole telling her dad. "Okay Sheyenne, I'll stay out of it but if you need me I'll be here. I love you honey. It will all work out." John replies and I can hear his chair sliding across the floor. I make it to the end of the hallway and turn the corner to walk into the kitchen at the same time John is turning to walk down the hallway. "Good morning John, How are you today?" I ask. "I'm great Xzavier. How are you?" He asks as he comes to a stop beside me. "I'm good Sir. Hope you have a great day." I say as he continues to walk down the hallway. "Good morning Nicole. How did you sleep last night?" I ask hoping she didn't sleep well either. "Morning Trent, I slept fine. Are you ready for an adventure today?" She doesn't look like she rested fine. She has dark circles under her eyes. "Yes, I'm up for a day of fun. What do you have in mind?" I reply as I'm fixing my bowl of blueberry oatmeal. "I'm not telling. Just make sure you wear swimming shorts. When I'm done working I'll come by and get you." She tells me as she's standing up to clean up her breakfast plates. I come to stop in front of her. She looks gorgeous without makeup and her hair is pulled in a ponytail. I can lose myself in her hazel eyes every time I look at her. I lean in and give her a quick kiss on the lips. Damn her lips are soft and plump. This quick kiss will have to do for now. She releases a soft sigh when I pull away. "Great, can't wait to see what you have planned for us." I tell her when she walks away to put her dishes in the dishwasher. "See you in a little while." She says as she leaves the kitchens and walks to her office.

Nicole

I tossed and turned all night long last night. I
couldn't stop thinking about how it felt to have Trent near
me. For five years all I've done is dream about the man
who was now in my reach. All I had to do was ask him in
last night and I could be waking up with him. Damn it!
Why does this have to be so difficult. These thoughts keep
playing through my head all morning long while I was
getting ready. Since I didn't sleep well I decided not to run
this morning. By the time I got to the kitchen everyone else
has already eaten and dad is last one in the kitchen. I grab
a bowl and walk over to the stove where I find grits. I take
the butter, my bowl of grits and my cup of coffee and sit
beside dad. Dad is finishing reading the morning paper like
he does every morning. He sits down the newspaper down
and turns his head to look at me. "Good morning Honey.
Are you okay? You look as if you didn't sleep well." He
asks with a questioning look. "I'm fine dad, I've got a few
things on my mind but don't worry I'll be okay." I smile and
reply as I stir the butter in my grits. "Your mom has
informed me who Xzavier is. Do I need to have a talk with
him? Dad asks with a stern look. "No dad I've got this
under control. There's nothing to worry about. Please let
me handle this in my own way." I tell him. I'm giving him a
pleading look hoping he will understand. "Okay Sheyenne,
I'll stay out of it but if you need me I'll be here. I love you
honey. It will all work out." Dad tells me as he is getting

up from his seat. Dad leans over and kisses me on top of my head. He would do that when I was younger as a way to help calm me down. Dad knows me really well and it's hard to hide things from him.

As dad is walking down the hallway, I hear him and Trent speaking to each other. I hope Trent didn't hear our conversion. Trent walks over to the cabinet to get a bowl. "Good morning Nicole. How did you sleep last night?' He asks. I'm not letting him know I didn't sleep. He looks like he didn't either and that makes me feel better. "Morning Trent, I sleep fine. Are you ready for an adventure today?" I ask as I'm finishing my coffee. "Yes, I'm up for a day of fun. What do you have in mind?" He replies as he is filling his bowl with oatmeal. Trent starts walking toward me. "I'm not telling. Just make sure you wear swimming shorts. When I'm done working I'll come by and get you." I tell him as I'm cleaning up my breakfast plates. By the time I stand Trent has stopped in front of me. He has a little stubble on his face and his eyes have a sleepy look to them. I didn't think Trent could be any sexier but I was wrong. He leans in and gives me a quick kiss on the lips. I love his soft kisses. I release a soft sigh when he pulls away. "Great, can't wait to see what you have planned for us." He tells me as I walk away to put my dishes in the dishwasher. "See you in a little while." I say as I leave for my office.

Chapter 15

I'm walking past Sasha's office on the way to mine when I notice Sasha is working as well this morning. "Good morning Sash." I say as I walk in the door and take a seat in front of her desk. Sasha looks up from her computer. "Morning Shy. So how are things going?" She asks. "It's been crazy." I say as I lay my head back on the seat and close my eyes. "You look like you haven't slept at all. Were you up all night rolling around in the sand with Xzavier?" She snickers at me. "Actually it's the exact opposite. I didn't spend the night with him. I couldn't sleep because all I could think about were his soft lips. I have no idea what I'm doing Sash. Then to top things off, Jasper showed up at dinner last night. He wanted to see if we could go for a walk." I say with a long sigh and run my hands through my ponytail. "Shy, have you slept with Xzavier again?" She asks. I reply with a shake of my head. "Shy!" She replies as she shakes her head. "I know Sasha that wasn't the best idea but I can't help the way he makes me feel. It's like I'm complete when he and I are together. I think I could really be in love with him. We have the best time and I feel whole. I felt our connection that first night five years ago." I tell her. "Well, you have a lot to consider when it comes to Xzavier. So you need to think long and hard about your choices before you make them. How did Xzavier act when Jasper was around?" She asks as she is getting up out of the chair. "Yeah, I know Sash. He acted normal. I thought I saw a flash of emotion but can't be for sure. He did ask about my relationship with Jasper. On another note, I started making a list of Things To Do for the Clouse Wedding. Liv will be here Wednesday. Can you and I meet Tuesday afternoon, so we can be prepared for our meeting with Liv." I ask as I'm getting out of the chair to head over to my office. "That's a great idea. I should be done in the kitchen by one if that's a good time for you." She responds before we split and start walking in different directions. "That's fine with me. Were you able to get in touch with you friend Lee to see if he could help out with the wedding?" I ask before I walk off. Sasha has this look in her eyes of longing. Wonder what the deal is with this guy. "Not yet. It's the beginning of the month, so he will be at the base for training drills all weekend. I just emailed him right before you came in my office. He'll either call or email me back once he's done with training drills. I'll let you know once I have an answer. If Lee isn't able to help, I do have another plan. Have a fun day today. I'm going to assume you will be spending it with Xzavier." She says while we're standing at my office door. "Yes, I have plans with Xzavier. Let me know if I need to help with anything. Have a good day Sash." I tell her as I turn to walk into my office. "Bye Shy, have fun today." Sash yells over her shoulder.

I walk over to my desk and sit down at my desk to start my computer. I need to review the work schedule for today and make sure we're covered for the weekend. I open the scheduling books for the different activities we offer and spend time reviewing each department to insure our guest will receive the best services. I also take the time to review supply request for each department and place my weekly order for supplies. By the time I finish a few hours have passed and it's getting close to lunch. I call down to the boat dock so I can set everything up for the day I have planned. "Hi Max, its Sheyenne, will you please make sure mine and dad's Jet Skis are ready. A friend and I will be taking them out today." I ask when Max picks up the phone. "Hi Ms. Anderson, yes I'll have them ready in thirty minutes. Is there anything else you need me to do?" He asks. "No Max that'll be it for today. Thank you." I reply before I hang up. I've decided that Trent and I will spend the day riding Jet Skis in the cove designated for family use only. I call down to the kitchen to speak with Mollie. "Hi Mollie its Sheyenne, will you please prepare a picnic lunch for myself and a friend. Have it delivered to the private beach hut say oneish." I ask. "Yes, Ms. Anderson I'll take care of that. Is there anything in particular you would like to have?" She asks. I have no idea what type of food Trent likes to eat. He did enjoy the sub sandwich he had last night. "Yes, please make sure there are various meats, all the fixings and bread for sandwiches, fruit, water, and sweet tea to drink." I tell Mollie. "Yes, ma'am I'll make sure the basket is there by one." Mollie replies right before she hangs the phone up. Okay, with that taken care of, I need to get ready and stop by to get Trent on the way to the boat dock.

I'm standing in my closet trying to decide which bathing suit to wear. It's a nice warm sunny day so I decide to wear my light yellow two piece. The top ties in the back and the around neck. The bottom ties on each side. I slide on a pair of torn blue jean shorts and sleeveless t-shirt to wear over my bathing suit til we reach the hut. I put my sunglasses on and leave the house so I can get Trent from the private living area attached to the Bed & Breakfast. I walk in the back door to find Mom and Dad sitting at the kitchen table. They seem to be in the middle of a conversion when I walked in. "Good morning." I say as I walk to the hallway that leads to Trent's room. "Morning baby, you look like you're ready for fun in the sun?" Mom asks. "Yes, ma'am I'm going to show Xzavier the island today." I stop and say to her before I continue down the hallway. I walk down to the guest room that Trent is staying in and knock on the door. Trent is on the phone when he answers the door. He motions for me to come in but I mouth that I'll be waiting in the kitchen for him. Before I turn around and walk back to the kitchen, I take a minute to look Trent over. He's wearing a white t-shirt with green swim shorts. He's so cute and I can't wait for him to take his shirt off so I can see that sexy chest of his. I turn and start walking back up the hallway when Trent call's my name. "Nicole." I stop and wait for him to catch up with me. "Hi gorgeous." He whispers in my ear when he's standing beside me. I turn my head to look at him and whisper back "Hi sexy. Are you ready for some fun?" Trent has the biggest grin on his face. "Being with you is all I need." He says as he kissed my cheek. I smile back. "You know how to say all the right things." I say back when he leans back from the kiss. "It's more than words. It's the truth Nicole. I enjoy our time together. It almost killed me when you didn't invite me in last night. I've dreamed of you for so long that being that close and not being beside you was awful." His reply causes me to release a soft gasp. "Trent." But before I could say anything else mom started walking down the hall. "Hope you guys have fun today. Remember it's supposed to be really hot today and there is a chance of showers this afternoon." She tells us as she walks past. "Thank you, mama. Love you." I reply. "Love you too." I hear her say before she disappears into the living room.

Trent grabs my hand. "Let's go. I can't wait to see what you have planned for today." He says as he starts walking forward. I have to start walking with him since he has a hold of my hand. We wave at dad who is stilling sitting at the table. He gives a wave and a smile. Trent doesn't let go of my hand while we walk down to the boat dock. I'm still in shock from his earlier comments to care. When we make it to the boat dock, I see Max standing on the dock. "Hi Max, is everything ready to go?" I ask when we get closer. "Yes, Ms. Anderson it is." He gives me a strange look when he notices Trent and I are holding hands. Max has worked for my parents for many years. He's like a grandpa to Sasha and I. He doesn't say anything to me but he does give me a smile which I return. "Thank you Max you're wonderful. Max this is Xzavier. Xzavier this is Max. He has worked for my parents for many years." Both men shake hands and say nice to meet you. "Xzavier make sure you take care of my Shy. She can be a handful at times." Max tells Trent as he walks past us. "Yes, Sir I plan to." Trent replies. I stand there shaking my head at their exchange.

"Okay Trent, I need to know if you know how to operate a Jet Ski." I ask as I'm pointing to dad's Jet Ski. "Yes, I do. It may have been a while since I've ridden but I think I can remember how it works." He answers as he is climbing on the Jet Ski. "Great, follow me and we'll go spend the day on the private beach that is used by family only. We have a beach hut there and I've requested a picnic basket be delivered around one today." I tell him as I sit down on my jet ski and turn the key to start it. I hear Trent start his jet ski. I make sure my sunglasses tightly secured and my hair is still in a ponytail before I take off. I look over to see if Trent is ready and wave for him to follow me. I start off slow so I can make sure Trent gets use to the Jet Ski. All of a sudden I see Trent fly past me and jump the wave that's coming toward us. Oh yes, he definitely remembers how to handle a jet ski. I pick up speed and jump the next wave. We continue passing each other and jumping the waves as they role in.. I wave my hand and signal for Trent to follow me. He turns the Jet Ski so he can come up beside me. We're both a little wet from jumping the waves. I would like to take off my shorts and shirt so I can be more comfortable. I turn so we can head to the private beach. I press the accelerator harder to make the Jet Ski go faster. Trent follows beside me never leaving my side no matter how fast I'm going. This is fun and relaxing. We make it to the beach in a few minutes. I slow down so I can ease the Jet Ski onto the sandy beach. Trent follows my lead and does the same. We climb off the jet skis and walk up to the beach hut. "This is a really nice place Nicole." He says as he is looking around the beach. "Yes, it's a nice little get away for the family. We can come down here to get away and relax. Don't get me wrong we can hang out at the beach around the Bed & Breakfast but then it's hard for us to relax. There is always someone needing something. Here we can get away from it all." I explain as I'm walking into the hut. The hut isn't big but it has enough room for a couple of people. There's a bathroom, small kitchen, sitting area, and even a futon bed.

"Sasha and I would come down here a lot when we were younger. It was our way of not being in the way. Mom and dad actually had a phone installed just in case Sasha and I needed anything while we were here." I tell him while I'm sinking my cell phone up to the stereo system. Luckily I have a water proof phone case. "From the outside this hut doesn't look like it would have this much room." Trent says as he looks around the room. His eyes stop on me when he notices I'm removing my clothes. "Holy shit Nicole you look amazing in that bathing suit." Trent barely manages to say when I'm finished undressing. "Thanks, what do you want to do now? We could ride the jet skis some more, go swimming, or we could just sit on the beach and enjoy the sunshine. We have about an hour or so before the picnic basket will be delivered." I ask as he starts to remove his shirt. Damn I want to rub my hands up and down his chest. Trent walks over to me when he has his shirt off and stops right in front of me. "What I have in mind isn't anything you mentioned." He states right before he puts his hand on my face and pulls me into a kiss. He starts slow but it quickly turns into a deep passionate kiss. I lean into the kiss when I wrap my hands around his neck. Trent moves his hand from my face to my waist and pulls me up against him. I can feel a hard ridge through his shorts. I break our kiss. "Trent." I manage to say while I'm trying to catch my breath. ""Sorry Nicole, I needed to kiss you." He tells me. Trent puts his forehead against mine. "Seeing you in this bathing suit knocked down my last little bit of will power I had left. I know you want to take this slow. It's just that it's been five years since I've felt this way." He tells me between the soft kisses. "Trent I understand exactly how you are feeling but there things we need to talk about. Five years is a very long time." I tell him as I'm stepping out of his embrace. "I want to spend the day with you and get to know you better. I'm not saying there isn't a chance for that activity." I say with a grin. Trent grins back and answers. "I agree so let's ride the jet skis some more. That was really fun." "Okay, let's go before lunch gets here. I'm going to beat you back to the jet skis." I yell to him as I'm running out the door. Before I know Trent is running beside me and trying to grab me so he will beat me. Before we can make it to the jet skis, Trent has tackled me and I'm trying to fight him off. Trent is laughing at my attempt to get him off of me. I'm finally able to wrap my legs around his waist and flip him over. His surprise shows on his face. I begin laughing with him. By the time we get up we're both covered in sand. I reach over to brush the sand from his face. It hits me like a ton of bricks that I'm falling deeper in love with this amazing man. I've been lying to myself thinking I would be able to keep this slow with him. I get off Trent and reach my hand out to help Trent up. "Come on let's get this sand off us and go for a ride." I pull Trent toward the water. I leave him standing on the beach and run into the water. The water is warm and feels goods. I dunk down so the next wave will wash the sand off. I come out of the water to see Trent watching me. He breaks eye contact and runs in the water. He runs far enough so he can dive into the water. I turn just in time to see him go under the wave. He pops out of the water a few minutes later. The sun is glistening off his wet body and I can see every muscle when he pushes his hair off his face. Trent swims back to me. "Are you ready to ride?" He says as he stands. "Yes, do you want to ride together or separately?" I ask as I turn to walk back to my jet ski. "Together is fine with me. I'll drive first." Is all I hear when he runs past me. I try to catch him but he's already on the Jet Ski when I get to him. He's laughing when I climb on behind him.

Chapter 16

Just as I wrap my arms around his waist, Trent gives the Jet Ski gas and we take off. He heads farther out into the ocean so we can jump the bigger waves. We've been riding and jumping waves for a while when I notice someone standing on the beach, I tap Trent on the shoulder to get his attention. He turns his head and I tell him to head in because our lunch has arrived. Trent turns the Jet Ski toward the beach. Once we're close enough I see Mollie standing near the water. Trent parks the Jet Ski on the beach and I walk over to Mollie. "Thank you Mollie for bring the basket down for us." I tell her but I notice she is staring at Trent as he is getting off the Jet Ski. I shake my head. Mollie turns to look at me and grins. I smile back. "You're welcome Ms. Anderson. Please let me know if you need anything else." She turns to leave just as Trent stops to stand beside me. "Come on I'm hungry." I say as I start walking toward the hut. Trent follows without saying a

word. Mollie has sat the basket on the table in the kitchen.
Trent walks over and starts pulling the food out. We have
plates and glasses in the cabinet so I pull a set out for each
of us. "Man there's a lot of food in here." Trent is saying
when I set the plates down beside him. "Yeah I didn't know
what you liked to eat so I asked for a variety of items, I
remembered you enjoyed the sandwich you had last night.
There should be several different types of sandwich meat,
bread, fruit, and sweet tea." I move the basket once Trent
is through getting everything out. "A good sandwich is one
of my favorite foods to eat and I loved the glass of sweet tea.
We're do you want to sit and eat?" He asks as he is making
his sandwich. "How about we set at the table on the porch
and enjoy the view of the beach." I reply as I'm making my
sandwich. "That sounds great." Trent and I complete our
sandwiches, pile our plates with fruit, and fix a glass of tea.
I lead us out to the small picnic table on the porch. We sit
down at the table and eat for a few minutes in silence.

"Nicole, I bet it was amazing growing up on the
island." Trent states as he takes a bite of watermelon.
"Yeah, it was fun but there were times it had its
disadvantages. Dating was never easy." I snickered back.
I reach over to pick up a piece of pineapple and see Trent
shaking his head. "I bet your dad had fun. I would pick
my daughter's date up at the dock in Madison and drive
him to the island. We would have a nice talk on the way.
Then I would give the two of them a ride back to the dock.
Waiting up for your daughter to return from her date would

have a whole new meaning." He says between laughs. "I can tell you it's not fun." I say before I eat a piece of watermelon. I'm lost in the thought imagining Trent with a child and didn't see Trent get up. "Earth to Nicole." I finally hear Trent say. "Sorry I was lost in thought. What did you say?" He smiles at me. "I wanted to know if you wanted more tea." Trent is holding my glass up. "Yes, that would be great." Trent walks back into the hut with our glasses. I'm staring at the beach when I hear Trent sit my glass back down beside me. "Thank You." I say when I turn my attention back to Trent. "You're welcome." He replies as he sits back down. We continue to eat the fruit and drink our tea. "So do you want to ride some more?" I ask when I eat the last piece of strawberry. "Yes, I do but I think we need to wait since we just ate. Let's walk down to the beach. My mom loves seashells and I would like to get her some." He tells me as he finishes his glass of tea. "Sounds like a great idea. I'll put the food in the refrigerator and clean up our dishes, while you sit here and enjoy the view." I tell him as I get up from the table. I grab the empty glassed and dirty dishes and walk into the hut. I put the remaining food in the small refrigerator and wash our dishes.

I finish putting the clean dishes up and turn to leave and notice that Trent is standing in the doorway watching me. "What are you doing?" I ask him. "You're so beautiful and sexy. Plus you told me to enjoy the view." Trent says with a soft laugh. As I walk past him to leave the hut I smack him on the arm. "You know I was talking about the ocean." Once I walk past him. "Yeah I know but I enjoyed watching you more." He says as he turns to walk with me. All I can do is shake my head at his response. "Are you ready to walk on the beach and find your mom a few seashells?" I ask as I reach for my sunglasses that I left on the table. "Yes after you." Trent and I walk down to the beach. When we reach the beach we each begin looking for seashells. There is very little conversation while we're looking for seashells. Every so often Trent would show me a seashell he found or I'd show him one that I found. We both had a handful of seashells when I found a conch shell buried in the sand. "Trent come here and look at this conch shell." I yell to him as I squat down and begin moving the sand from the part that's buried in the sand. Trent comes up beside me and squats down to help me finish digging the conch shell out of the sand. When we finish digging the shell up we're surprised to see it's a fully intact conch shell. "Nicole this shell is beautiful; I believe this is the first time I've actually ever seen a complete conch shell found on a beach." Trent tells me as we stand up. I walk down to the water to rinse the shell off. Once clean we can see the shell is a beautiful cream color with a little gray. "I bet your mom will love this shell and all the others we've gathered for her." I say once I stop beside him. "Yes, she will. I think we have enough so are you ready to ride the Jet Ski?" He asks. "Yeah let's go put these up and we'll ride for a while." I say as we begin walking back to the hut.

Trent

Nicole is beautiful, fun, smart, and just all around amazing. After I kissed her earlier all I've wanted to do is kiss her again. I watched her while we were picking up seashells and damn all I've thought about is kissing those soft lips again. We are walking back to the beach so we can ride Jet Skis again. Nicole is playing with the keys to the Jet Ski and talking about the amount of seashells we found. "It's my turn to drive." Nicole reminds me as we pull her Jet Ski back into the water. "How can I forget?" I smile back.

Nicole climbs on and tells me. "Get on Trent. I promise to go easy on you." I climb on and wrap my arms around her waist. "I can handle anything you can do." I whisper in her ear. She snickers at my comment. Nicole starts the Jet Ski and pulls away from the beach. The wind has picked up and the waves are bigger than they were earlier this morning. Nicole turns the Jet Ski towards the waves and gives it gas so we can jump the incoming waves. I hear Nicole laughing each time we jump the waves. Her laugh is intoxicating. All this jumping and bouncing is causing Nicole to rub against me. I'm not sure I can control myself. It took all I had this morning when she was rubbing against my back. We continue to ride the waves for the rest of afternoon. The waves have slowed down and Nicole turns the Jet Ski off so it can float around in the waves. I lean in to whisper in her ear. "Nicole I've enjoyed myself today. I haven't relaxed liked this in years and I owe it to you." I kiss her ear and begin running my fingers in a circular motion on her belly. I move my hands up to cup her breast and begin to massage them through her bathing suit. "I know you want to take this slow but I've wanted to touch and kiss you all day long." I tell her as I'm kissing her neck. "Trent." Is all she manages to say with a deep sigh. Nicole leans her head back to give me better access to her neck. I slide my hands under her bikini top so I can feel her soft breast. Nicole's nipples are hard and I begin to rubbing them. I remove one hand from her breast, lean her back against me, and slide my hand into her bikini bottoms. As my fingers touch her, I hear Nicole release a soft moan. I turn her head so I can kiss her. Damn she feels so good. Nicole takes one hand and places it on my cheek while we kiss. Nicole breaks our kiss so she can untie her bikini top tied around her neck. Her top falls down to expose her breast. "Trent let me turn around?" She asks.

I remove my hands and Nicole turns around so she is facing me. The lust and need I feel is shining back at me from Nicole's eyes is driving me crazy. She sits downs and places her legs over my thighs and smiles at me. Nicole unties her bikini bottoms, slowly removes them, and turns around so she can tie them to the steering handle. As she is leaning back I softly kiss her side and then her breast. She turns to face me again and I pull her in for another kiss. She slowly slides her tongue over my lips and I deepen our kiss. I feel her hands sliding down my chest and into my shorts. When Nicole slides her fingers over my cock, my cock hardens more, and I moan into her mouth. "Trent, take these shorts off." She asks between kisses. Nicole slides her legs off of me and I turn so both legs are on the same side of the Jet Ski. Nicole assists me by sliding my shorts down as I lift my butt up off the seat. Nicole takes my shorts and hangs them on the steering handle. I straddle the seat to face Nicole again. "Trent slide up to the middle of the seat." Nicole tells me as she slides back on the seat. I slide forward as Nicole slides her legs over my thighs and slides her body against me. My hard cock is pressed up against her and she begins to rub herself on me. I lean her back so I can suck and nibble on her round breast. I move from one breast to another and I feel Nicole slide closer to me. "Trent let me slide you inside me." Nicole manages to say through her heavy breathing. I let her breast go and put my hands on her waist to help steady her. She lifts up enough to where the head of my cock is pushing against her entrance before she slowly slides down. Nicole is so wet that I easily slide in. She sits down in my lap and begins to ride me. I can't move since I'm trying to keep us steady. Between the motion of the waves and Nicole I'm sinking deeper into her. "You are amazing and you're sending me over the edge. I can't control myself when I'm with you." I say as I suck her nipple in my mouth. "Trent, I've dreamed of you for so long that it's hard to believe you're actually here. To be in your arms now is a dream come true. I'm afraid I'm going to wake up to find out all this has been one amazing dream." Nicole says. Nicole's honesty is so refreshing. I've dealt with so many ladies whose only reason for being with me was the money I've made or the connections I have. I slide back to where I'm sitting at the back of the seat and lay Nicole down so I'm on top of her. I begin moving fast and hard to push both of us to our orgasms. "Oh shit Trent. Right there that's it." I can tell she's about to cum when she tightens around me. Just as she squeezes around me again, I feel her release and it sends me into my own orgasm. I continue sliding in and out till we've both come down from our high.

Nicole

I'm trying to catch my breath after the incredible sex I just had. I've fooled around on the Jet Ski before but this is way above anything I've done in the past. Trent is outstanding no matter where we are. My legs are still wrapped around Trent so he hasn't moved off of me. "If I don't move soon my ass will be sunburned." Trent says with a snicker. "That would make it very uncomfortable for you to sit." I reply back with a laugh. Trent sits us both up and kisses me. "My dear Nicole, I'd suffer through a sunburned ass to be with you. How about we jump in the water and get cleaned off. I think we can put our bottoms back on too while we're in the water." Trent tells me as he ties my bikini top around my neck. I look around and notice the waves have pushed us closer to the beach. "Sounds like a great idea." I tell him as I stand. I jump off the Jet Ski into the ocean. I come back up just in time to see a naked Trent dive into the ocean. That's a site I'll never forget. I grab my bikini bottoms, put them on, and climb back on the Jet Ski to wait for Trent. When Trent climbs back on the Jet Ski he's fully clothed. "We've been riding for a while now, do you want to go back to the beach and get something to drink or eat?" I ask Trent over my shoulder. "Yes, that sounds like a terrific idea." He replies as he leans in to kiss me on the cheek. I start the Jet Ski and head back to the beach. Trent helps me pull the Jet Ski back on the beach. We walk back to the hut and head straight to the kitchen. Trent walks over to the refrigerator as I reach in the cabinet for cups. "Do you want tea or lemonade to drink?" I hear Trent ask "Lemonade would be fine with me." I reply. Trent brings the lemonade over to the counter and pours us a glass. "Thank you. What would you like to do now?" I ask between swallows of lemonade. "How about we relax on the beach for a while?" Trent replies. "I'm fine with that. There are a couple of lounge chairs in the storage cabinet located at the end of the porch. If you will grab them, I'll get us a couple of towels just in case we decide to swim." I tell him as I walk toward the bathroom. I hear Trent walking to the door.

I grab the suntan lotion on my way out of the hut. By the time I make it out of the hut I see that Trent is finishing setting up the last chair. He looks ups and watches me as I walk to him. He has the biggest smile pasted on his face which causes me to smile. Oh man how I love his smile. I stop right in front of him. "Will you put suntan lotion on my back?" I ask as I put the towels in the chair. "Yes, I would be glad to." He replies. I hand the bottle to Trent and turn around. Trent squeezes lotion in his hand and hands the bottle back to me. He starts at my shoulders and works his way to the top of my butt. It feels really good to have his hands rubbing my back. I start laughing and squirming when Trent slowly slides his fingers up and down my sides. "Ah, you're ticklish." He softly whispers in my ear. I heard the enjoyment in his voice. Trent continues to tickle my sides and I laugh even harder.

"I love to hear you laugh. It's so sexy and sweet." Trent tells me as he wraps his arms around me and pulls me to him. "I love being in your arms and getting to spend the day with you. It's been a while since I've had this much fun." I tell him as I turn to face him. I can tell by the shine in his eyes he's feeling the same way I am. I lean in and give him a soft kiss on the lips. "I'm going to finish putting the suntan lotion on and relax for a while in the lounge chair. Are you going to join me?" I ask. "I'm going to go for a swim in the ocean. The blue water looks so inviting." He tells me. "Okay, I laid a towel in your lounge chair." I tell him while I finish rubbing suntan lotion. I finish just in time to watch him as he walks into the water and dives in. I stretch out in the lounge chair and lay on my stomach. I feel asleep at some point because I've been woken up by the cool water drops hitting me. "Trent, please stop dripping water all over me." I say without opening my eyes. "I'm not dripping water on you. It's starting to rain. Guess your mother was right about the chance of showers this afternoon. Come on let's get to the hut before the heavy rain gets here. I see it coming across the ocean." I hear Trent say as he folding up his lounge chair. I get up fold mine and we begin walking back to the hut. Just as we're almost there the bottom falls out and we begin jogging the last few steps. We set the lounge chairs on the porch next to the front door as we walk into the hut. "I'll get us some towels so we can dry off." I tell him as I walk toward the bathroom. I grab two towels and take one to Trent. He stands in the door frame watching it rain. "I never knew watching rain could be so relaxing. The sound of the rain hitting the roof and the trees around us is soothing. These are things you don't hear in New York." Trent tells me as he takes his towel and begins to dry himself off. "Yes, I have to agree with you it's very relaxing to hear. I think we may have an extra pair of shorts if you would like to change. It looks like it may be a while before it stops raining." I tell him as I begin to dry myself off. "Yeah it would be nice to get out of these wet shorts." He replies. "If you'll go look in the bathroom there are several pairs of shorts in the cabinet. You should be able to find a pair that fits you." I tell him as he walks to the bathroom. "Thanks." He tells me over his shoulder. I'll wait for him to finish and then I'll change.

Chapter 17

While Trent is in the bathroom changing, I decide to take out the food that was left after lunch. I'm a little hungry and I bet Trent is too. "Trent, are you hungry?" I ask when I hear the bathroom door open. "Yes, I am." He replies as he's walking towards me. He's changed into a pair of blue shorts and he decided to go shirtless. "Great, I've taken the leftovers out of the fridge and arranged everything on the bar. Go ahead and fix yourself something to eat while I get changed." I say as I walk past him. I always have an extra set of clothes stored at the hut. I grab my shorts and shirt from earlier and walk into the bathroom. I decide to put on another bathing suit top under my shirt. When I walk out of the bathroom I see Trent standing on the porch talking on his phone. I pick up the stereo remote when I pass the stereo system on my way to the kitchen. Just as I make it to the kitchen Trent's getting off his phone and joins me at the bar. "Man the rain sounds so good hitting the top of the hut. It never sounds this good at home." Trent tells me. "Yeah it does sound really nice. You can never tell how long it's going to rain. These afternoon showers are unpredictable." I tell him as I start making my sandwich. I look over and he is making his own sandwich. I reach for the stereo remote once I have my sandwich made. "I'm going to turn some music on. Is there anything in particular you would like to listen to?" I ask once I have the stereo on. "No, I like just about everything." Trent says as he is pouring his glass of tea. "Great I'll sync my phone to the stereo and let it randomly play music while we eat." I hit play but really don't pay attention to which song it plays first. Trent has already taken his seat at the bar by the time I sit down and begin to eat. We sit there talking and eating. Before we know it the sun is setting and it was still raining. "Man how long have we been sitting here?" Trent asks once he realizes it's starting to get dark. "I'd have to check my phone but it's probably about seven o'clock. It's still raining to so it may be best if we just spent the night here. Are you okay with that?" I ask as I put our dishes in the sink. "Yeah I'm fine with that." Trent replies and I can hear the smile in his voice. Trent comes over and helps me finish cleaning up. Just as we are finishing up Trent ask. "Dance with me? I love this song." This causes me to stop and really listen to what is playing. "Yes, I agree Thinking Out Loud by Ed Sheeran is a beautiful song." I say as he takes my hand. I remember how it felt the first time he and I danced together five years ago. He pulls me up against him and wraps one arm around my waist. We begin swaying to the music and before I know it he is leading us into a Waltz. "Do you know how to Waltz?" Trent has leaned in and softly asked me in my ear. "Yes, it's been a few years since I've done the Waltz but I think I can still do it." I reply back. "Great follow my lead." He replies just as he takes his first step. I follow his lead and before I know it we are spinning, twisting, and moving around the hut in complete sink with each other. When we finish dancing I realize the song playing currently is Like I'm Gonna Lose You by Meghan Trainor. There's no telling how long we were dancing. Dancing with Trent has reminded me of how much I love to dance. Trent is a great dance partner. "We're did you learn to dance?" I ask. I'm still in Trent's arms. He hasn't let me go even though we've finished dancing. My back is up against his chest and he has both arms wrapped around my waist. "Well I have an aunt who was a professional dancer. From the first time I can remember seeing her dance I was in love with dancing. So when my aunt wasn't working she would teach me a new dance. By the time I reached high school I was helping her in her dance studio. After high school I went on to college and graduated with a Business Major but dancing was what I really wanted to do. So that's when I started my own company. Did you take dance lessons? You're a wonderful dancer yourself." He asks as he begins to sway us side to side. "Thank you. I had few dance lessons when I was little but nothing like you had. I basically learned from watching movies or videos. Dancing was one of the reasons Brandy, Megan, and I became friends. They were in the few dance classes I took. We'd work on dance routines when we spent the night together so by high school we were a great team. That's how we all three became the lead dancers for the dance line." I tell him as I lay my arms over his. I hadn't realized to now that we were standing at the door. The moon is shining bright as it's peeking out from behind the clouds and with the rain pouring down it is a beautiful site. We continued to stay there for a while longer swaying and watching the rain. I don't want this night to end, I feel complete when I'm in Trent's arms.

     I feel Trent leaning forward to kiss me on the cheek. After he kisses my cheek he leans in to whisper in my ear. "Nicole, I believe I've been in love with you since the first time I saw you. I've thought of you so much over the last five years. For the longest time after our night together I would see you everywhere. When I got closer to them I'd realize it wasn't you. This all feels like a dream and I don't want to wake up ever if it is." I don't realize that I was holding my breath until a soft gasp escapes my lips. I turn around so I can look into Trent's beautiful blue eyes. "Trent, I feel the exact same way. I feel complete when I'm in your arms." I tell him as I stand on my tip toes so I can place my lips on his. I feel Trent's arms tighten when I put my hands in his shaggy hair and pull him closer so I can deepen the kiss. After a few minutes, he breaks our kiss to look me in the eyes. I see a fire so hot it would burn down anything in its path. "Nicole, I want to make love to you." He whispers against my lips. "Yes, please." Is all I manage to say before he picks me up carries me to the bed. He puts me down and goes over to where the light switch is and turns the lighting down. The soft glow from the moon, lights the hut, and the sound of the rain hitting the roof is a very romantic setting. I hadn't realized to now that it was raining again. Trent stops in front of me and reaches up to untie my bikini top from around my neck. Then he reaches under my shirt to untie the last tie and pulls it out from underneath my shirt. He drops the bikini top on the floor just as he begins kissing my ear. I'm running my hands through his hair as he begins kissing from my ear down my neck. I feel his hands sliding under my shirt to grab my breast. He begins massaging them as he continues to kiss my neck. Trent slides his hands down grabs the bottom of my shirt and pulls it up and over my head. My nipples are hard and Trent begins sucking on my left nipple as he kneads the right nipple with his hand. He slowly kisses his way from my left breast to my right one. He sucks and nibbles on my right nipple as he kneads the left one with his hand. When he bites my right nipple I release a soft moan and I feel myself become wetter than I was already. I feel Trent as he slides his hand down my belly to undo my shorts. Once he has them unbutton he slides he hand down the front. When he discovers I didn't put a bikini bottom he released a moan of pleasure. He slides one finger into my wet folds and this time I hear him release a soft growl. "Damn you're soaking wet." He says against my breast that he's been teasing with his tongue. I feel him slide one finger deeper into my entrance and I moan with pleasure. He slides his hand out of my shorts to pull them down my legs. I step out of them and I'm standing completely naked in front of him. I step a little closer so I can remove the shorts he has on. I slowly remove his shorts. I hear him gasp when I softly run my fingers up and down his hard shaft. Trent closed what little distance there was between us and I feel his hard cock pressing up against my belly. I place my hands on his shoulders and pull him down on the bed with me. Our kisses start of slow and easy but become faster and more passionate. Trent grabs my legs and puts my feet on the end of the bed so he can spread my legs wide open. He slowly kisses his way up my body until he's on top and I feel the head of his cock at my entrance. Trent slowly slides his cock inside and with every inch he's filling me completely. He begins sliding slowing in and out as he kisses me. Our hands are linked above our heads. His slow movements begin to change to faster and harder rhythm. With each push he's sending me closer to an orgasm. Trent lets go of my hands so he can grab my legs and wrap them around his waist. This change in position allows Trent to go deeper and I wrap my hands around his back. Before I know it I'm digging my nails in his back and matching his moves. Our movements become faster and harder, Trent raises himself up so he can grab my breast and I run my hands down his arms and over his chest. "Trent harder I'm almost there." Is the only statement I can mange as he pushes his cock harder and hits the exact spot to send me into an explosive orgasm. As soon as I reach my release I feel Trent as he does too. Trent lays down on me while he's still inside me. I slowly rub my hands up and down his back as he plays with my hair. We lay that way for a while trying to catch our breath and slow our heart rates down.

When we've finally gotten our breathing under control, Trent slides his cock out of me and reaches for the bed sheet. "Nicole, lift yourself up so I can pull this down for us." He says just as he starts pulling the sheet down. Once he has the sheet down enough, he crawls in behind me and covers us up. Trent pulls me closer so my back is up against his front. We're lying on the same pillow and one arm is under my head while the other one is wrapped around my waist. I've laid one arm over the arm that's wrapped around my waist and my other is holding the hand that's at my head. "Trent, I don't want to leave this hut. There's been so many nights that I've wished for a night like tonight. Can we spend the day tomorrow at the hut?" I ask. "I would love to spend the day with you here at the hut. I have no plans other than spend the day with you." He replies and I feel the smile on his face. "Let's get some sleep. We've had a very eventful day today." He says right after he gives me a kiss on the cheek. I'm not sure I can sleep but to my surprise I fall asleep pretty quickly.

Chapter 18

It takes me a few minutes to remember where I am as I wake up. I start to move and realize Trent is stilled snuggled up against me. "Good morning beautiful." He says when he realizes I'm awake. Trent moves the hair from my face and runs his fingers softly down my neck and shoulders. The soft kisses that follow his fingers feel wonderful. "Good morning. How long have you been awake?" I reply as I take his hand in mine. "I've been a wake for a little while. I didn't want to move and disturb you. I was enjoying watching you sleep. You are so beautiful when you sleep." He tells me between kisses. "Thank you." I say as I turn over to face him. I run my hands through his messy bed head and lean in to kiss him. Trent leans in to meet me. I give him a soft peck on the lips. "So what do you want to do today?" I ask as I pull my lips from his. "How about we go for a swim and just lounge around the beach today." He replies. "I'm fine with that." I answer with a huge smile on my face. We both get out of bed at the same time so we can retrieve the clothes we discarded at the end of the bed last night. Once we're both dressed we head out to the beach for a swim. Trent and I spend several hours swimming, laying on the beach, and riding jet skies before I put the hammock up for us to relax in. Trent climbs on first and I lay between his legs. "Today has been perfect, Nicole. I haven't had this much fun in years. I've actually been able to relax." He tells me as we are start swinging in the hammock. "I'm glad to hear that. I have a question. Have you ever been deep-sea fishing before?" I ask. "No I haven't." He replies. "Well, would you like to be one of the first guests to try out this newly offered service here at the Bed & Breakfast? This is something I think will add to the appeal of the Bed & Breakfast but I haven't put it out for the public yet. I wanted to have a few of our guest give it a test trial and give me feedback before it's listed as a new service. When we get back to the main house this afternoon, I'll contact Joseph so he can take you out tomorrow morning." I tell him. "I'll be happy to try it and give you my feedback. What time will I need to be ready?" He asks has he continues to rub his fingers through my hair. "I'll let you know once I talk with Joseph." I reply. The feel of him rubbing his fingers through my hair is so relaxing that it's making me sleep. Before I know it, Trent is waking me up. "Nicole, it's getting late and I think we need to head back." "Sorry I feel asleep. Yeah, I agree we do need to head back.

I have a few things to take care of before work tomorrow." I reply as I begin to set up and get out of the hammock. We head back to the hut to make sure everything is turned off. I'll ask Ashley to send someone down tomorrow to clean up and replace the drinks and snacks we ate today. I put my shorts and shirt on over my bikini and make sure any other clothes are put in the dirty clothes hamper. "Trent, if you want to change back into your shorts from yesterday. You can put those shorts you have on in this dirty clothes hamper in the bathroom." I tell him as I walk out of the bathroom. "Thanks, I'll do that." He says as he passes by me on his way to the bathroom. I walk around into the kitchen to make sure the stereo system is turned off. I pick our cell phones up off the counter and walk to the door to wait on Trent to finish. I'm staring at the waves rolling up the beach when Trent walks up behind me and wraps his arms around my waist. He leans in and whispers in my ear. "I have no idea where this is going between us but I want to find out. This has been a dream weekend but I know we must get back to reality. Nicole, I'm falling in love with you. I can't recall if I've ever felt this way before about another woman." I lean my head back against his shoulder. "Trent, I've dreamed about this weekend so many times that I don't want to leave either. I'm falling in love with you too. Actually if I'm honest with you I think I've been love with for the past five years." I reply in a soft whisper. Trent turns me around to give me the sweetest kiss filled with all the passion he's feeling. Trent breaks the kiss and takes my hand so we can walk down to the beach. We have one more quick kiss before we jump on the Jet Skies and head back to the main house.

Trent and I are pulling up to the dock when I see Samuel coming our way. "Good afternoon Samuel. Will you please fill both the Jet Skis up and put them up for me?" I ask him when he stops in front of me. "Yes, ma'am I'll take care of them for you." He replies as he climbs on my Jet Ski. I look over to see Trent tying his Jet Ski to the dock. I wait for Trent to finish so we can walk back to the main house. Just as we make it back to the walk way that leads to private living area and my home, I stop before walking on to my house. "Trent I'll see you at supper. I have to get things together for work in the morning. I've got to call Joseph and find out what time y'all will have to leave in the morning if he's able to take you out in the morning. I'll let you know at supper tonight what Joseph said." I say as I come to a stop. "I have a few things I need to do for my meeting I have Friday morning. I'm looking forward to the deep-sea fishing trip in the morning. It sounds really interesting." He says as he takes my hand to place a soft kiss on top of it. "See you later." Is all I can say when he lets my hand go and I turn to head to my house. I hear Trent say "Until later then." We go our separate ways for now.

Trent

It's only been a few hours since we got back but it feels like it's been days. I've tried to keep myself occupied by reading emails, calling my parents to check on them, and taking care of a few last minute items for my meeting on Friday but nothing works for long. All I keep remembering is how right it felt to be with Nicole. Actually holding Nicole in my arms while she slept was a hundred times better than any fantasy I've had during the past five years. I'm taken back to how I felt the first night we spent together. I keep recalling how right it felt to hold her, kiss her, and to make love to her. I feel that she claimed a part of my soul that first night together and when she left she took part of me with her. Yes, there have been other women since that night but no one has made me feel the way Nicole has. No other woman has made me feel complete and completely undone at the same time. Nicole connects with me on an emotional level and I'm not sure I can understand it. Hell, I'm not sure I want to understand it. Being with her is like pouring gasoline on a fire. Just thinking about her is making me hard. I turn my attention back to the contract I've been trying to review for the last thirty minutes. I look over the last few changes and add my notes so Anna can make the additional changes. I email the document to Anna and close my computer. I glance down at my watch and notice it's almost dinner time. Nicole and her family have dinner together and I can't wait to see her again. I think I'll see if she would like to take a walk on the beach after dinner. I really need to discuss a few things with her but I can't do it tonight. I'll have to before I leave on Thursday. I get up from the desk and walk to the bathroom to get a shower just as my phone rings. I grab the phone off the dresser and continue walking so I can turn the shower on. Samantha hears the water running so she makes the call a short one. She just wanted to let me know she would be back in New York by Thursday. Samantha is one of the models I use in my dance videos. She happens to be a great dance but works more as a model. I set the phone on the counter and hop in the shower.

It doesn't take me long to shower and get dressed. The excitement of seeing Nicole in a few minutes is more than I can bare. I leave my room and as I'm walking up the hallway I hear Nicole and her family talking and laughing. Just the sound of her laughter has my heart racing and images of her beautiful smile are turning me on. When I make it to the kitchen, Nicole and her sister are sitting at the dining table laughing. Her mom and dad are standing at stove fixing their plates. "Good evening everyone." I say so they will know I'm there. A round of. "Hi Xzavier." Comes from everyone. "Come fix you a plate." Lilly instructs me as she turns to walk to the table. "We have fried chicken, baked potato, turnip greens, sweet potato casserole, creamed corn, and cornbread. For dessert we have your chose of pecan pie or chocolate cake." John tells me as he finishes making his plate. "Man everything sounds good can't wait to taste everything." I say as I grab a plate off the counter and begin to fix my plate. "Xzavier how did you like the private hut and beach?" John asks as I sit down next to Nicole at the table. Out the corner of my eye, I can see Nicole's cheeks blush slightly and her smile widens at the mention of the hut. "It's really nice place to get away and relax. I hated to leave. I was able to find several beautiful seashells for my mom. She collects them. Nicole found a complete conch shell that I know she will love." I reply back. "That's really nice of you to think about your mother and collect the seashells for her." Lilly tells me. "Thank you, my brothers are always telling me, I'm a mama's boy." I reply between bites of food. "So you have more than one brother?" Sasha asks. "Yes, Jeremiah is my younger brother and then there's Luther who is my older brother. Jeremiah is a lawyer and Luther is a Doctor. Jeremiah is the first of us to get married. Luther and I have been too busy with our careers to even think of marriage. Mom is happy that one of us has finally decided to marry. Now she feels she will have a chance to have grandkids." I tell them. "I bet your parents are proud of all three of you. Y'all have great careers." Lilly replies as she finishes eating. "Yes ma'am they are. Mom loves giving us a hard time. She thinks we should have already started a family." I say with a laugh.

We've all finished eating now and have been sitting around the table talking. "The food was amazing. Thank you for allowing me to join you." I say as I get up from the table. I reach over and pick up Nicole's dishes and set them on top of mine. "Trent you don't have to do that. You're our guest." She tells me as she puts her hand on mine to stop me. I can tell by the look on her face that she just realized she call me Trent instead of Xzavier. "It's the least I can do." I tell her as I walk past her and pick up Sasha's plate. John has already picked his and Lilly's plates up. "Xzavier will you help me clean the kitchen?" John asks as I hand him the dishes I've collected. "Yes, sir I would be happy to help. Ladies you all sit there and relax." I say. "Y'all are such a gentleman." Lilly tells us. "Thank you." I say as I turn around to help John with the kitchen. John and I talked about several different things as we clean. He tells me about the history of the island and why his parents first decided to open the Bed & Breakfast here. John also shared his hopes that the Bed & Breakfast will be there for many years to come. He explained how Nicole and Sasha have helped with the success of the Bed & Breakfast since they have started managing. That reminded about the deep-sea fishing trip.

"Nicole, what time do I need to be ready in the morning to go deep-sea fishing?" I ask as I finish wiping off the counters. "I spoke with Joseph when we returned. He stated that he and Beck would meet you on the dock at seven thirty in the morning. Since this will be your first time going deep-sea fishing, they want to make sure you have a thirty minute fishing lesson. I thought that was a wonderful idea. So for all guests who have never been deep-sea fishing, this thirty minute class will be required before they can actually leave the dock. There are a couple forms that I need for you to review and sign before you actually meet Joseph and Beck on the dock. The Bed & Breakfast has contracted with Joseph and Beck to provide these services so we need to have signed liability forms on file. I have the forms in my office so you accompany me my office at 7:00 to sign the forms. I'll walk to the dock with you once all the forms are signed." She replies. "You've never been deep-sea fishing before?" John asks. "No sir I haven't. I've heard friends talk about it but I haven't been myself." I tell him as we walk back to the table where the ladies are still seated. "My calendar is open tomorrow so I think I will join you, if that's okay with you Xzavier." He asks when he comes to a stop behind Lilly's chair. "I would like that sir." I tell him as I'm sitting down in the chair next to Nicole. John leans down and gives Lilly a kiss on the side of the cheek. He grabs the back of the chair and helps Lilly up. "Goodnight everyone, we're retiring for the night. Trent I'll see you in the morning." John and Lilly walk out of the kitchen as we goodnight. "Guys I have got to go myself. I need to review the menu and supply order for the kitchens. Hope ya have wonderful evening." Sasha says as she gets up from the table and walks to the restaurant. "Goodnight Sash." Nicole and I say at the same time.

"I guess it's only us now. Would you like to take a walk?" I say as I turn to face Nicole. "Yes, I'd love to. I know exactly where we can walk." She says as she starts to get up from the table. I stand and help her up. We walk out the kitchen, take a left and head toward a walking trail. We walk in silence both lost in our own thoughts. This has been a dream come true weekend. I've been able to finally spend time with the woman who owns my heart. I've got to figure out how I'm going to keep her in my life. Nicole has owned my heart since the first time our eyes connected five years ago. I can't take this space between us so I reach for her hand. I slide my fingers between hers and I feel her tighten her grip on my hand. I pull her hand up and kiss the back of it. "Where are we going?" I ask just so I can break the silence between us. "I wanted to show you the new addition to the Bed & Breakfast. The construction should be completed at least two weeks ahead of scheduled." She replies just as we reach a newly built walkway. "I can't wait to see it." I tell her as I pull her a little closer. We walk a little further and I can see the new buildings. Both buildings are smaller versions of the original house. "These are gorgeous Nicole." I say as we get closer to the houses. "Thanks, we are really proud of them. For the past few years we have been booked all summer and had to turn registrations away. We're hoping this will help. Also it's an added bonus for weddings. Jasper did a great job with the design. Come I want to show you the honeymoon cabin. The construction on the cabin is complete. I need to get with the interior decorator to finish it up." She tells me as we walk past the two buildings. We walk a little further past the two building to a cove. The cove is surrounded by beautiful trees and flowers. Just through the trees you can make out the cabin. The closer we get the more beautiful the cabin and the cove become. The cabin sits just off the beach. We're still holding hands as we enter the cabin. The cabin is one floor with an amazing open floor plan. As you come in the front door you can see the beach and ocean through the large French doors at the back of the cabin. The kitchen, living room, and dining area are in the huge area. Off to the left of the kitchen is a door. Nicole walks over to it and opens it. Behind the door is the master suite with attached bathroom that has a large whirl pool tub and large shower. Nicole leads me to the back porch that has access to the beach. We stop at the porch railing and I release her hand so I can stand behind her. "Nicole this is amazing. This is a terrific place to spend your first night as husband and wife." I tell her as I wrap my arms around her waist and place a soft kiss on her cheek. "Thank you. That was my thought when we started the process of adding the new additions. Jasper and I worked closely to make sure this was the most romantic spot for a new couple." She tells me as she leans back on me. I feel a pang of jealously as she talks about her and Jasper working together on this cabin. Nicole continues to tell me about the different things that were done for the new additions but the fact that she and Jasper spent time together in the beautiful spot is not setting well with me. I could tell that Jasper is in love with Nicole when

I saw him with her the other night. I nod and respond to her but I can't really tell you about anything she has been explaining. I squeeze Nicole closer to me and kiss her on the neck. The beach below is small but it's just perfect for couple to have privacy. "Would you like to go down to the beach?" she asks. "Yes I love to." I reply as she takes my hand and leads us to stairs that goes to the beach. The stairs are lighted just enough to see where you are stepping but not enough to light up the area around the steps. I just noticed the sun has started setting. "We also decided that it would be a great idea to have a small hut tucked away in the corner of the beach. This way the couple wouldn't have to worry about carrying items up and down the stairs. There will be lounge chairs, a hammock, and anything else that would be useful on the beach." She tells me as we make it make it down to the bottom of the stairs. We stop on the last step and she points out the hut she was just telling me about. She slides her flip flops off as she steps onto the beach. I do the same. The sand is still warm for the sun. I bring her hand up to my lips and place a soft kiss on her knuckles. She smiles at me and I can see the twinkle in her eyes. There's a slight breeze coming off the ocean but it just warm enough to be standing on the beach without a jacket. I take Nicole's hand turn her around and her back is against my chest so I can whisper in her ear. "This is an amazing place to spend your first nights as a married couple. The sound of the ocean and the breeze as it blows gives off the water provides the most romantic feeling." I feel her lean into me so I start swaying back and forth in a slow dance. She is moving with me. It's the most intoxicating feeling and I turn her to face me. With my lips inches from hers I whisper. "Nicole, I knew I had strong feelings for you when we meet five years ago. After these few days, I know those feelings were the beginning of the love I have for you." I feel her warm breath as she releases the breath she was holding. Within seconds she closes the few inches between our lips. The kiss is soft and slow. Nicole slowly breaks the kiss but only moves her lips a few inches away and her eyes are sparkling more than earlier. She whispers back. "Trent, I've loved you in my dreams for five years. Those dreams hold nothing on the love I've felt as well these past few days." "Nicole, before I leave on Thursday we'll figure out how to make this work. I know it may not be easy but I will give it my all to be with you." I tell her as I pull her in my arms. I continue the slow dance from earlier. There's nothing better than having Nicole in my arms as we slow dance to our own music from the ocean.

Chapter 19

Nicole

I slowly roll over so I can turn my alarm off. I don't want to get up because the dream I was having was amazing. Trent and I were back on the private beach at the new newlywed cabin. We danced until sunset and we couldn't see any longer. He and I laughed and joked as we walked back to the main house. I still felt his lips on my lips for hours after he kissed me goodnight. I sit up with a sigh and glance at the clock to see its five thirty. Trent and my dad are going deep-sea fishing today. Trent has to sign the consent and other liability forms so I decide to run on my treadmill instead of the beach this morning. Sasha normally runs with me so I grab my phone to send her a text letting her know I'm not running on the beach this morning. I get dressed and step out on the back porch where my treadmill is and set it for a forty minute run.

After my run I take a quick shower and dressed for the day. I walked to the main house to have breakfast with everyone.

As I walk in the door I hear everyone laughing. "What's so funny this early in the morning?" I ask as I come through the back door. "Dad was just telling Xzavier about the time he went deep-sea fishing and the baby hammer head almost pulled him in because he wasn't paying attention." Sasha replies. I laugh at the thought because I remember the story. I look at Xzavier. "You should ask him to show you the pictures. The site of him hanging on to the boat and the fishing pole is hilarious. Beck was able to reach dad before he went over. Dad didn't let go of the fishing pole and was able to pull the hammerhead shark in." I say laughing. "I meant that shark wasn't going to beat me." Dad said. I look back at the stove and see Ms. Betty Ann standing there stirring something in a pot. I walk over to see what she is cooking. "Good morning Ms. Betty Ann." I say as I come up beside her. "Morning sweetheart. How are you this morning?" She asks as she turns the eye off. "I'm fine." I reply as I look in the pot to see what Ms. Betty Ann was stirring. She is cooking grits. "Grab a bowl and I'll scoop you some." Ms. Betty Ann tells me. I do as I'm told and place the bowl next to the stove. "Xzavier is a really nice young man. His features remind me of someone but I can't say for sure right now who he reminds me of." She finishes pouring grits in my bowl. "He is a very nice guy." I reply but make sure I don't comment on her last statement. Ms. Betty Ann just gives me a sly smile because she knows who he reminds her of but she won't say it out loud. I lean over and give her a kiss on the cheek. Just as I lean back from the kiss I whisper thank you and head over to the table where everyone else is sitting. I sit down and start putting the butter, salt, and pepper in my grits when I hear Xzavier ask. "So how did this idea to add deep-sea fishing come about?" "Well I've known Joseph and Beck for a very long time. We all went to school together. After high school both Joseph and Beck enlisted in the Army. After serving several tours in the Middle East, they came back to Madison hoping to start fresh. I happen to run into them one day while I was in Madison. I asked them if they still loved to fish. I explained to them that I was thinking about adding deep-sea fishing as a service and wanted to know if they would be interested in becoming the deep-sea fishing guides. Luck would have it that Beck's uncle had given him a boat that would work perfect for deep-sea fishing. So we've been working on the contracts while the guys worked on the boat to make sure it was in great shape. Once the service has been tested to make sure we've worked out all the logistics, the deep-sea fishing will be listed as a new service offered to all guest and anyone else who would like to book a trip. Joseph and Beck wanted to also use this as a way to help other Veterans, so deep-sea fishing trips will be free all Military Veterans." "That is truly amazing and I'm happy to be a part of the experience." Xzavier replies.

Dad and Xzavier continue to talk about the upcoming fishing trip.

"Sash, can we move our meeting to today to go over our notes for the meeting with Liv on Wednesday?" I ask as I get up to put my dishes away. "Yes, I'll have time later today. I need to make sure the kitchen has everything it needs to for the week." Sasha replies as comes up beside me at the sink. "Great I'll be back in the office after I make the rounds to see how everyone is doing this morning. Xzavier are you ready to head to my office to sign the consent forms?" I ask as I start walking back to the table. "Yes, lead the way." Xzavier answers me. Xzavier and I walk to my office taking the back way through the main kitchen. "I printed the forms out last night when I got back home from our walk. The forms should still be on the printer." I tell him as we come into my office. I turn the lights on in my office and walk over to the printer. I hear the door shut behind me. The printer is located on the wall next to desk. I turn around so I can give Xzavier the forms. He takes the forms out of my hands and lays them on the corner of the desk. "I've wanted to do this all morning long." He says just as his lips touch mine. The kiss starts off slow but turns passionate as he places his hands on each side of my face. I place my around his neck to pull him closer to me. I'm unsure how long we've been kissing but we finally have to separate so we can breathe. "Well good morning to you." I say with a smile. I give him a quick kiss on the lips and turn to pick up the forms.

"Please read over these and let me know if you see any changes we need to make." I say as I hand him the forms. He takes a seat in one of the chairs in front of my desk. It doesn't take him long to read over the forms. "These are pretty straight forward and simple to understand." He states as he's signing. "Good, are you ready to head to the dock? Even though its ten after seven, I know dad, Joseph, and Beck are already there." I tell him as I lay the forms in front of my computer on my desk. "Sure I'm ready but first I need another one of these." He finishes his statement by kissing me again. "I could do this all morning but you need to get on a boat and I have work to do. How about we have dinner tonight?" I ask as we walk to the door. "I'd love to." He replies. We leave my office and walk to the dock where the boat is docked.

We chat about how beautiful the morning is and how nice it is to hear the birds singing. As we reach the dock I see dad talking with Joseph and Beck. "Good morning guys. Are y'all ready for the day?" I say as I come to stand in front of Joseph. "Hi Shy. Yep ready to go and catch a big one." Beck replies as he picks me up and gives me a bear hug. Beck sets me down and Joseph gives me a hug as well. I turn to Xzavier and see he's smiling at us. "Joseph this is Xzavier. This will be the first time he's been deep-sea fishing. Make sure to take it easy on him. He's from New York." I smile at the guys and turn back to Xzavier. Xzavier extends his hand so he can shake Beck and Joseph's extended hands. "I'm excited for the opportunity. I would also like to thank you both for the sacrifices you've made to help defend our Nation." Xzavier tells them. "Thanks man, so you've never been deep-sea fishing before?" Beck asks while Joseph is still loading the last of the equipment onto the boat. "I've had friends that have but I've been so busy with my business that I haven't taken a lot of time for myself." Xzavier replies. "Well we have all day to show you what you have been missing." Joseph replies as he comes to stand next to Xzavier. "Joseph, did the kitchen already deliver the food for today?" I ask. Supplying all meals during the fishing trips is a part of the agreement with Beck and Joseph. "Yes, Sash was waiting for us when we docked the boat this morning. She even helped us put everything in the galley." Beck responded as he handed Xzavier a life vest. I took that as my queue to leave. "Xzavier, hope you have a terrific time. Beck. Joseph. It's always good to see you." I say as I'm walking over to my dad who has just walked back to the group after talking with Bob. "Dad, please don't let the fish out do you and have a great boys day out at sea." I tell him with a laugh as I give him a hug and kiss on the cheek. He hugs and kissed me back. "Thanks sweetheart. I'm sure we'll have a blast." He tells me as he walks past. I turn one last time to wave at the guys before I leave to make my morning rounds.

I happen to run into Megan as I enter the reception area. "Good Morning Meg. How was your weekend?" I ask as I come up beside her. We continue walking to Megan's office. "We actually had a wonderful weekend. Celica and Luke both had open day for recreation t-ball and Matt had a softball game to coach." She tells me just as we reach her office door. Sounds like y'all had a busy weekend." I replied. "It was but tomorrow night Matt's parents are keeping the kids so Matt and I can have a long overdue date night." She has the biggest grin on her face when she tells me. She takes a seat at her desk to review her schedule for the day. I just shake my head and laugh at her. Matt and Meg were high school sweethearts. They've been married for five years and have two beautiful kids. Luke is turning four in August and Celica turned three this month. "Oh no I remember one of the last times y'all had a date night. We have beautiful Celica to show for that night." I say jokingly. She just grins back at me. "So how was your weekend?" She asks. Now she has turned to face me directly. "It was a good weekend. I spent Saturday at the family beach." I reply. I can tell by the look on Megan's face that she knows there is more to the story. "Yes, Trent spent the day with me. We rode Jet Skis and ended up staying in the hut Saturday night." I reply to her unanswered question. "So things are good between you two. Have you been able to talk?" Megan asks. I sigh before I answer her question. "No we haven't talked about anything. We've both started but we stopped each other. Trent and I both didn't want to ruin the fun we were having. Trent promised we would figure things out before he left on Thursday." We heard the bell over the entrance singling that Megan's first customer of the day had arrived. We both get up from our seats and start walking to the front of the salon. As we walk the short walk to the front Megan turns to face me and says. "Shy, I hope everything goes okay when you finally get to sit down and talk. I know how much you care for Trent and I hope he returns the feelings." I give her a quick hug and reply. "Thanks Meg. Have a good day."

I make it back to my office to finish my morning work. I'm not sure how long I've been working when Sasha walks in. "Hi Shy, are you ready to go over everything for Wednesday's meeting." "Hi Sash, yeah give me a couple of minutes to complete what I'm doing." I reply as she sets down in the chair in front of my desk. I finish up the last little bit of work and retrieve my notes from the other night out. I look up and notice that Sasha also has a notebook in her lap. "So Sash, did you get an email back from your friend in Savannah?" I stand as she starts to reply and motion for her to walk over to the table next to my desk. "Yes, Lee emailed me back last night. He's happy to help out with this. I'm heading to Savannah Wednesday so I can meet with Lee and go over Nikki's menu." She finishes telling me as she sits down in the chair next to me. She seems really excited or maybe it's anxious about seeing this guy. I've got to find out what's going on. "Okay, I know there's a story here. Tell me about Lee." Sasha leans back in the chair and looks away before she turns her eyes back to me. She takes a deep breath as she begins to answer my question. "Do you remember when I attend cooking classes in Atlanta about two years ago?" I nodded my head in response and she continues. "Well Lee was attending the same class. Lee can be a very intimidating man when you first meet him. He's six foot three and built. Because of his stature I admired him from a distance but there were several times he and I were paired together during classes. During those times I learned he was a very smart and a gentle man. He was home on leave and the cooking classes were a part of his therapy to help deal with the PTSD he was suffering from. The more time we spent together the more I learn about him. Cooking reminds Lee of summers he spent in the kitchen with his grandmother. Lee and I would hang out even when we weren't in class. The more time I spent with him the more I began to care for him. I felt he was beginning to care for me to but he was holding himself back. Then one night he and I were at my apartment having supper. We had spent most of the evening in the kitchen joking and laughing. Let me just say that the joking and laughing turned into a kiss that sent a rush through me. A kiss has never made me feel the way Lee's kiss did. I know you're wondering and yes that kiss lead to more. It was an amazing night. He was gentle with me because he was afraid he was going to hurt me since I'm smaller than him. I'd never felt so treasured by man before and it was overwhelming. After that night we spent as much time together as we could but I was only able to get him to spend the night with me twice. He was afraid that he would have a flash back and hurt me. He'd been in therapy for about a year but with him still on active duty the therapy was an ongoing process." Sasha stopped for a minute as if she was remembering something but continued before I could ask what she was thinking.

"We had about three weeks of classed left. Lee and I had a wonderful weekend checking out the different restaurants in Atlanta. When I got to class Monday morning Lee never showed up. I had begun to worry because Lee was never late for class nor did he miss class. As I was cleaning up my station at the end of the day, Chef Wong come over and asked that I see him before I left that afternoon. When I finished up I headed straight to Chef Wong's office. Chef Wong was sitting at his desk when I entered the office and he asked me to sit in the chair in front of his desk. Of course I was wondering what Chef Wong wanted to see me for but it wasn't long before he explained. He started by giving me praise on how well I was doing in class but he knew I would do well because I was already a great chef. We talked a little longer about the restaurant here. Before I got up to leave Chef Wong held out an envelope that had my name on it. Chef Wong told that Lee came to see him before class that morning and asked him to give the envelope to me at the end of the day. I was a little taken back by that but I took the envelope from Chef Wong and said my goodbyes. I made myself wait until I made it back to my apartment before I opened the envelope. Luckily my apartment wasn't that far from the school. I couldn't wait anymore so as soon as I had shut the door to my apartment I opened the envelope. I read the letter twice to make sure I read everything correctly. Lee was called back to duty early. He had received the call late Sunday night after he returned back to his apartment. He wasn't sure when he would be back from this mission but he wanted me to know that our time together meant a lot to him. He gave me his email address and asked that we stay in touch. Shy the next three weeks of class felt so empty without him. I hadn't realized til that point I was falling in love with Lee. I wasn't sure if Lee felt the same.

Over the last two years I've keep in touch with him. He has also become a very dear friend during that time and I didn't want to lose that. I haven't seen him in two years but I know my feelings for him haven't changed." I now understand that it's worry and hurt that I see in her eyes. Sasha is trying to hold back the tears that have moistened her eyes. "Sash, why haven't you told me about Lee before now?" I ask when it looks like she isn't going to continue talking. "Shy, I finally understood some of what you had been going through. The difference with me was the fact I was able to talk with the man I fell in love with. I didn't want to add to your hurt because you loved a man that was more of dream." She answers. I lean over and take her hands in mine and tell her. "Sash you should have never keep this to yourself. You should have talked to me. So what are you going to do?" "Shy, the whole time I'm there I'll have to make sure I keep our interactions to friends. In our emails we've never talked about us. Lee's letter didn't give any notification that he thought of me as more than a friend. He's also never said anything about being in a relationship with anyone now that he's no longer on active duty but I know he has to have someone. Women always paid attention to him when we were out. I've been telling myself this is just another business transaction with someone who is also a good friend." She stops and I ask. "Are you going to be okay working with him?" "Yes, I'll be there a couple of days. I've booked a hotel room in Savannah. Lee owns a restaurant on Bay Street that isn't far from the hotel. I've wanted to go back and visit Savannah for a while now so this works out well. You know they have some wonderful seafood restaurants. I'd also like to take a day and ride over to Tybee Island. Plus I can't wait to see his restaurant." She shakes her head and puts a big smile on her face. "I trust that you know how to handle this but know if you need me I'll be there for you." I tell her as I lean over and give her a hug. "I know and I think that's enough about me. We need to make sure we have everything ready for Wednesday. I've brought a list of things I thought we needed to go over." She tells me as she places the notes on the table in front of her. I take that as the sign we need to get down to work.

Before we know it we had spent hours going over our notes and combining them to insure we have everything ready for Wednesday. Sasha had lunch delivered so we can continue working without interruptions. While we were talking about the number of temp employees we'd need for the party I decided to get Sasha's insight on the total of new employees we'll need to hire when the new rooms were open. We're both excited to show Liv the island and the many different ideas we have. Hopefully between what Liv has and what we've come up with this will be an amazing event. One item that we haven't discussed with Liv or Nikki happens to be the rehearsal dinner. Since the wedding party will be here the night before we need to have that menu. Hopefully Liv will have this with her. "Shy, you know if this goes well that this is only the beginning." Sasha states as she leans back in her chair. "Yeah I know. This is what we've been working for. I'm excited and hope that mom and dad are. We've watched them work hard to bring the Bed & Breakfast to what it is today." I reply as I push my chair back from the table and turn to face her. "I'm glad we've been able to help them build on what they've already accomplished. Speaking of dad, have you heard from him since they left this morning?" She asks. "No I haven't but I didn't expect to. You know how dad gets when he's fishing." I smile at her when I reply. "Wonder how Xzavier is doing? How are things going with him? Y'all have been spending a lot of time together." Sasha comments. "I hope he's having a great time. I think deep-sea fishing would be a great addition to the activates we already offer. I've enjoyed spending time with him. The more time I spend with him the more I fall in love him. I knew there was something there when we first meet five years ago. I'm not sure what will happen when we actually sit down to talk about what's going on with us. Right now I'm just enjoying my time. I've dreamed about having this for so long that I'm sure this is all a dream and I'll wake up soon." I reply with a soft laugh. Sasha shakes her head and laughs when she replies. "Well let me just say this is one strange dream if it is." We sit laughing and enjoying the moment.

"Who's working in the kitchen this afternoon? I want to order dinner for Xvaiver and I tonight?" I ask just as we both start to get out of our chairs. "Mel is working tonight." She tells me. "Great he makes amazing pizzas and that's what I wanted for tonight. I'll go by there later and talk with Mel." I reply just as I make it back to my desk. I happen to glance at the clock and notice its two o'clock in the afternoon. The guys are supposed to be back around five this afternoon. "He'll be happy to make you whatever you want. I've got to get back to my office and make sure the kitchen will be taken care of while I gone for a few days. See you later Shy." Sasha says as she walks out of my office." "Bye Sash." I say just as she leaves. I sit down at my desk and wake my computer. I need to go ahead an email the different employee agencies we use to help find new employees. I take the notes from Sasha and my meeting and send several different job descriptions, the number of permanent and temporary employees we'll need, and the dates the employees will need to work. We've used these agencies before so they have the already know the additional hiring requirements. I also send an email to

Ashley, our receptionist, so she can be prepare to handle
the calls when the agencies start to setup interviews.

   Before I know it the rest of the afternoon has flown
by. I leave my office with a feeling of accomplishment and
hope that our meeting with Liv on Wednesday will go well. I
wish Ashley a goodnight as I pass by the reception desk on
my way to the kitchen. It doesn't take me long to find Mel
when I make it to the kitchen. I tell him what I would like
to have for supper and ask if he can make it for me. "Yes,
ma'am I can have it all ready for you by seven. I'll also get
Mike to have everything delivered and setup so you will be
able to enjoy your dinner." Mel replies. "Thanks Mel.
You're the best." I tell him as I turn to leave. I haven't seen
mom since breakfast. So I leave the kitchen and head over
to mom's office to see how she's doing. I knock as I enter
mom's office. Mom is sitting behind her desk working on
her computer. "Hi mom, how has your day been?" I ask
just as I make it to the chair in front of her desk. She looks
up from the computer and smiles at me. "Hi sweetheart,
it's been a busy day but a good one. So did you and Sasha
get everything together for Wednesday's meeting?" She
asks as she leans back in her chair. I've sat down in the
chair that's right in front of her. "Yes, ma'am I think we've
got everything together. This is going to be one of the best
events we've held here." I tell her. "Yes, I can agree with
you. We've had several nice events but none of them can
match the size of this one. Nikki is our first high profile
wedding. I hope the wedding won't be to overwhelming for

our other guest." Mom states. "Sasha and I have discussed adding several additional staff for that day. Hopefully that will help insure that our non wedding party guest will not be affected. We're thinking that we'll have to double the staff for that weekend. Several of the wedding guests may stay a few extra days if they like it here. At least Sasha and I are hoping that will happen." I tell her. "I think your dad has gotten a few request already. He was telling me the other night that he's been receiving emails requesting the cost for additional days. I'm not sure anyone has confirmed the extra days yet." She says as she picks her phone up. "Mom, have you heard from dad today? I was wondering how the fishing trip was going." I ask when she has set her phone back down on the desk. "Actually that was him there. They're on their way back in. He expects they will be back by six. He sent me a picture earlier and they look like they were having a blast. Xzavier hasn't sent you a text?" She asks. "We haven't exchanged phone numbers. That hasn't crossed my mind to ask. I guess we'll address that and other items before he leaves on Thursday. He's told me we'd talk about everything then." I tell her as I lean up in the chair getting ready to leave. "Well I hope everything works out for the both of you. A lot of things can happen in five years and y'all have only spent a few days with each other." She tells me as she gets up from her chair and walks around her desk to stand next to me. I stand up to reach over and give her a hug and a kiss on the cheek. "Thanks mom, I love you. I've got a few things to take care of before Xzavier and I have supper tonight. See you later." I tell her as I make my way to the door. "Love you too sweetheart." I hear her say as I leave the office.

I spend the next hour getting everything else ready for supper. I finish setting up for supper and walk back to the main house just as dad and Xzavier come walking up the trail to the house. "Hi guys did y'all have a great fishing trip?" I ask as we come to stop at the steps. "Now Shy, you know I always have a great time when I go out with Beck and Joseph. Today was no exception. Xzavier fits in great with us. We had a blast and can't wait to go out again." He tells me as he stops to give me a kiss on the cheek and continue his way up the steps. "I'm really glad to hear that dad." I say with a laugh and a shake of my head. "So Xzavier did you have a great time as well?" I ask just as he comes to a stop in front of me. "I had a lot of fun. Those guys are beyond crazy. Now I know why your dad loves to go deep-sea fishing. Are we still on for dinner tonight?" He asks. "Yes, everything will be ready by seven. Meet me back here and we'll go eat." I tell him just as he steps a little closer to me. "Great I can't wait to finish the day spending it with you." He says in a whisper just as he places a soft kiss on my lips. His lips fill a little gritty from being out in the sun. When Trent pulls back from the quick kiss, I lick my lips and taste the salt he left on my lips. He smiles at me and turns to go up the steps. I watch him go into the house before I turn and start the short walk to my house.

I decide to wear a cute strapless summer dress that stops right above my knees. The dress is comfortable and looks really cute on me. The light green color and the small white flowers accent my tan skin. I stand in front of the mirror trying to decide how to fix my hair. I end up pulling my hair up into a ponytail that hangs down my back. I apply a small amount of face powder and lip gloss. Since I'm going for a comfortable look and feel for tonight I decide to wear a pair of white slip on sandals. I look over at my clock on the wall next to my door and see that I still have about fifteen minutes before I have to meet Trent. The walk to the main house doesn't take long and I enjoy the warm breeze along the way. When I almost make it to the main house, I see Trent walking around outside talking on the phone. He looks good. He's wearing light brown shorts and a light blue polo shirt. As I get closer he looks up and sees me. A big smile spreads across his face as he hangs up and puts his phone in his pocket. I come to a stop in front of him. "Good evening Nicole. You're looking beautiful and sexy. So what do you have planned for us tonight?" Trent asks as he leans over and gives me a kiss on the cheek. When he leans back I can see the sparkle in his eyes that I saw the first time we set eyes on each other. I want to lean over and give him a kiss on the lips but I'm very aware of where we are. I smile back and I can feel my cheeks warm from the blush that is spreading across them. "Thanks.

You're looking very sexy yourself. Are you ready to eat?" I ask. "Yes but I'm really ready to spend more time with you. Eating is a bonus." He replies with a sexy smile. I smile back at him and begin walking toward the new houses. Trent comes up beside me and takes my hand in his. "So the deep-sea fishing trip was fun I take it by the way you answered me earlier. Since that was your first time are there any changes that you would suggest?" I ask as we continue to our walk. "With it being my first time and not having anything to compare it to personally, I would have to say that everything was great. I've listened to my brothers and friends talk about their trips but I couldn't ever imagine it was as fun as it was. Beck and Joseph are amazing teachers. They explained everything to make sure I clearly understood what I was supposed to do. They allowed me to help with everything from setting up the fishing poles, baiting the lines, and they even allowed me to move the boat into place." He tells me. "Glad it went well and you had a great time." I tell him as we start to pass the two new additions. Trent gives me a look but he continues. "I can honestly say that I believe this will be a great added adventure for the Bed & Breakfast. It's also great that the fish caught during the fishing trips will be taken give to families who are in need. Joseph was explaining that he understood what it felt to wonder when you'd get your next meal. So he's decided to help the families who need it. Beck was telling me that they also plan to take fish to the local VA Hospital and serve the Veterans as a treat. Beck and Joseph are two great men that are willing to help everyone they can." He tells me as we come up to the front porch of the honeymoon cabin. I open the front door and lead us through as I reply. "Yes, those two guys have a heart of gold. It's amazing they aren't bitter due to the way they both were raised. Beck and Joseph have been friends for as long as I can remember. Both grew up without their dads and their moms worked multiple jobs so they could take care of their sons. Don't get me wrong their mothers did the best they could, but working as they did left the boys alone. Beck and Joseph were neighbors so they actually took care of each other. That's how strong their friendship is. Actually, now that I think about it they're more like bothers than friends. When Beck enlisted it was a given that Joseph would. As luck would have it both men were stationed at the same base. I'm not sure if they had been separated how they would have been." "Your dad seemed to very fond of them as well. He was always giving them praise and the boys were really happy that he was proud of them." Trent comments. "I think dad was one of the first male figures the guys had in their life. Dad met them one day while he was in town. They were sitting outside one of the shops staring at the food through the windows. I think dad was worried they were going to do something stupid so he took them in and bought them something to eat. As soon as they were able to help out here my dad put them to work. I think they were only thirteen when they first started helping out. Dad would give them small jobs to keep them out of trouble. Beck and Joseph's mothers were happy that dad had helped them keep the boys out of trouble. The older they got the more work dad gave them. The boys were paid for the work they did and it made them feel good to help their mothers out. That's how we all became good friends. Speaking of dad did he behave during the trip?" I ask just as we make it down the stairs to the private beach. I see that Mike has delivered everything that I asked for. "He didn't twenty question me about what my intentions were with you. We joked all day and had a great time. Wow what do you have planned for dinner?" Trent asks when he sees everything.

"Well I was thinking after you had spent the whole day fishing that maybe you would enjoy a picnic under the moon and stars." I turn and walk to where the blanket has been placed on the beach. On the blanket there are several pillows to sit on, a small flat mat so we can take our shoes off and not get a lot of sand on the blanket, and the food containers. We walk over to the blanket and I gesture for him to sit down with me. I reach over and pull the pizza from the carrier Mel put it in to stay warm. "I wasn't sure what type of pizza you like so I had Mel in the kitchen make a large pizza that was half meat lovers and the other half is supreme. There's sweet tea to drink, along with fudge brownies for dessert." I tell him as I continue to pull everything out of the containers. "Nicole this is amazing. I'm really at a loss for words. I've never done anything like this. You have no idea how bad I want to kiss you for thinking of this unbelievable dinner for us. I love both types of pizza so either one would be fine with me." Trent tells me as I make his plate and hand it to him. I make sure we each have a glass of tea as we begin to eat. We talk more about the day he's had and how he can't wait to do it again. He wants to plan a day with his brothers and dad. I explain that Sasha and I worked most of the day preparing for our meeting with Liv on Wednesday. Before I know it we've finished the large pizza and half of the brownies. "Nicole that was really good. That was a homemade pizza wasn't it?" He asks as he hands me his trash. "Yes, it was. Mel makes the best pizzas." I tell him as I finish cleaning up our trash and putting up the leftover food.

By the time we finish eating the sun has set and the moon is beginning to rise. There are a few stars starting to fill the sky. Trent takes a few of the pillows and lies back so he can look up at the sky. "Nicole the sky is beautiful. I know I've mentioned it before but I can't tell you how these last few days have meant to me. I've worked so hard the last five years that I haven't taken any time to enjoy life. I just keep pushing myself. Laying here listening to the waves, looking at the stars in the sky, and being able to share this with you has made me the happiest man. Come lie down beside me and enjoy it with me." He says as he reaches his hand out to me. I take his hand and lay down with him. I put my head on his shoulder and lay my hand across his chest. I can feel the rapid beat of his heart. "Trent, these last few days have meant so much to me as well." I tell him as I draw little circles on his chest. Trent leans over and kisses me on the top head. I'm not sure how long we lay there holding each other and just enjoying the moment. Trent has been rubbing my back with his one hand and holding my hand with his other. He lets go of my hand and lifts my chin up so I'm looking at him. "I hadn't realized until now how incomplete I've been. I knew that something was missing. No matter what I tried I felt a piece of me was missing. The feeling started the morning after we spent together. Nicole, I've been in love with you since that night." Trent finishes saying just as he presses his lips to mine to kiss me. I give into his kiss because I've loved him just as long. The kiss starts off slow but becomes more passionate the longer we kiss. I break our kiss, lift myself up, and throw my leg over him so I can straddle him. I sit there looking down at Trent and he sets his hands on my thighs. "Trent, I love you as well. There hasn't been a day since I met you that I haven't thought about you." I tell him as I lean down to kiss him again. I run my hands through his soft hair and deepen our kiss. Trent slides his hands up my body to pull me close to him. Trent breaks our kiss and kisses a trail up my cheek to my ear then down my throat to my collar bone. He takes his time kissing me. The soft feel of his lips is turning me on with each kiss. "Oh Trent, I want you now. You're driving me crazy with kisses." I say breathless. I begin breathing faster as the trail of kisses begins to work their way down to my left breast. Before I realize what he's doing he rolls me over on my back so he's on top of me. Trent never takes his lips off of me as we roll over. He pulls the top of my dress down to expose my breast and he continues his kisses until he takes my nipple in his mouth. While he is licking and sucking on my left nipple he kneads my right breast in his hand. I lift my back up to push breast further into his touch. I can feel how much he wants me through his kisses and the hardness that's pressing up against me. I begin rubbing myself against him and he releases a soft moan as he kisses his way from my left breast to my right. He gives the right breast the same attention he gave my left one. Trent's right hand grabs the hem of my dress and pulls it up to my waist. The next time I feel his hand he's rubbing the small piece of cloth of g-string that's covering my wet entrance. "You're so wet that this little patch of cloth is soaked." Trent tells me as he releases my right nipple and pushes the cloth to the side. I feel two fingers begin to rub me before he slides them into me. The slow easy pace is sending me closer and closer to an orgasm. Just as I think I can't take anymore he removes his fingers and begins undoing his shorts. "Nicole, nothing will ever compare to making love to you under this beautiful night sky. You're the other half of me I've been waiting on. I know we still have things to talk about but tonight it's just us and the love we have for each other." Trent whispers in my ear just as I feel the head of his cock at my entrance. The words Trent just spoke and the feel of him as he inches his cock inside me has left me speechless. I'm only able to show my pleasure and happiness with a soft moan. I lean up and kiss him softly. He makes slow strides sliding his cock in and out of me. I wrap my legs around his waist and begin to move in same slow steady motion. We continue this slow steady pace for what seems like for every. There are no words needed to explain how much we mean to each other at this moment in time. We kiss each other slow and easy with the same rhythm as our love making. The orgasm that was building with each steady slide of him inside me comes without a warning. Trent picks up his pace as he finds his release at the same time I do. He swallows my moans and cries of pleasure with a kiss. We lay there still connected as our heart rates and breathing try to return to normal.

Unsure of how long we've been this way I kiss Trent on the cheek and he turns his head so he's looking at me. The sparkle I love is shining in his blue eyes. Trent returns my kiss with a soft peck on the lips. "I could stay like this forever but it may become uncomfortable because of my weight on top of you. Also it may not be good for me to constantly have a hard on." Trent laughs as he kissed me on my nose and starts to pull himself out of me. I tighten my legs around his waist not letting him move. "Your weight doesn't bother me and I'm truly enjoying your constant hard on." I reply with a giggle as I begin moving my hips causing him to moan. "So I take it you're ready for round two." Was the reply I got as he pushed his cock deep in me. I sucked in a deep breath and released it with a moan. "Yep I'm ready." I let him know with a twirl of my hips. With my legs still wrap around him, Trent pulls us up into a sitting position. He's sitting back on his legs and I'm sitting in his lap with each move he pushes deeper and deeper into me. I begin riding him and he meets each of my thrust with thrust of his own. He sucks the nipple he has in his mouth at that time. Our love making is different this time but no less than it was a little while ago. I tilt my head back pushing my breast deeper in his mouth just as he slides against my sensitive spot sending me into another orgasm. The spasms from my orgasm send Trent into his as well. He lays us down just as we both are coming down from the high of release. He slides out of me and fixes my dress and his shorts before he lies down beside me. Trent pulls me up to his side and wraps his arms around me to cocoon me in his warmth. "I'm not ready to leave this spot. How about we lay here for a while listen to the ocean and watch the moon and stars move across the sky?' I tell Trent. "Nor am I ready to leave. I'd love to lay here as long as you want." He replies. So we lie there enjoying the beauty of the night.

Chapter 20

Trent

I'm woken by this beeping noise and realize there's someone sleeping next to me. As I slowly begin to wake the memories from last night fill my mind. The love Nicole and I made on the beach last night was amazing. The feel of her head resting on my chest this morning only adds to my feeling that she's meant to be mine. I look at the sky and notice that the moon is nowhere in sight. I don't want to move and disturb Nicole but I need to grab her phone to stop the beeping noise. As I move to reach for the phone Nicole opens her eyes. "Hi baby, sorry didn't mean to disturb you but your phone is going off. I was trying to reach it to silence it." I tell her as she rolls over and grabs the phone. Hi is her response as she stops the beeping noise and checks the time on her phone. "We sleep on the beach all night. It's five thirty in the morning." She tells me with a sheepish smile. "Wow. That's the best sleep I've had in a while. It felt good having you sleep next to me. Do we have to leave right now?" I ask as she lies back down next to me. "No we don't have to leave. I normally get up at this time so I can get my morning run in. I just sent Sasha a quick text to let her know I will not be joining her this morning." She replies as she snuggles in between my arm and left side. I squeeze her closer to me and kiss her on the top of the head. I link my hands together and hold her with a hug. "Can we stay right here all day and let the rest of the world pass us by?" I ask. Nicole begins laughing. "I was just thinking the same thing. I've dreamed of nights like last night and waking up in your arms that I'm not sure if this is a dream or not." I pinch her on the side. "Ouch, okay I'm not dreaming." She begins laughing and I laugh with her. "I just had to make sure because I would be very unhappy if this was all a dream. Life here is so much simpler than it is in New York. Don't get me wrong I love New York but the last few days have help me understand that we all need to take time to slow life down. I want more days like this one." I gently place my fingers under her chin to tilt her face up so I can look into those amazing hazel eyes. I lean down and place a soft kiss on her lips. I want her to see what I'm feeling through my eyes as I'm saying the words to her. "I love you, Nicole. I know we have things to work through but I feel we can." I give her another quick kiss on the lips. "I love you too. I feel the same as you. I've wanted and wished for you every day of the last five years." She replies as she kisses me back. "I hate to break this moment but I do need to get ready for work this morning. Tomorrow is a big day with Nikki's wedding planner coming to the island." Nicole pulls back sits up and pulls herself into standing position looking down at me.

The sunshine behind her head causes the red in her hair to shine which makes her look even more beautiful than she already is. She reaches her hand out offering to help me up. I take her hand and rise to my feet standing just in front of her. Because I'm few inches taller she has to tilt her head back a little to look at me. I can't resist it so I give her another quick kiss and pull up against me. "I've got a few things I have to take care of this morning as well. I have a meeting with a new client when I get back to New York on Friday. Can we have lunch today?" I ask as we start picking the pillows, blankets and leftover food up. "Yes, I would love that. I'll be in my office so when you're ready come and get me. I'll have one of the tables on the deck saved for us." She replies. "Sounds great I can't wait. It looks like it's going to be a beautiful day." I reply as we set all items we just picked up at the hut on the private beach. "I'll send someone down here to collect this and make sure it's cleaned and stored back in the hut." She tells me as we start our walk back to the main house. It's short walk so it doesn't take long for us to get back to the house. We stop at the door that leads into the private kitchen. "Thank you for a great night. I'll see you at lunch." I lean over and give her a kiss. She leans into the kiss. "Hope you have a wonderful morning. See you at lunch." She says as she turns to walk toward her home and get ready for the day. I watch her walk and just as I'm about to turn away she looks over her shoulder and blows me a kiss. Before I can do anything she turns back around and continues her walk. I still hope she feels the same about me when we talk on Thursday. I shake off those thoughts and go on into the house to get this day started. I'm ready to spend more time with Nicole.

Nicole

I barely remember getting ready this morning. I'm floating on cloud nine since Trent told me he loved me. Luckily I managed to dress myself in a one of my tan one piece jumpers. It's loose and cool for the warm weather. Breakfast with mom, dad, and Sasha was filled with dad telling us about the crazy things the guys did during the fishing trip. We laughed so hard at his stories. Trent didn't eat with breakfast with us. I was a little sad I didn't get to see him again but I knew we were having lunch together later today. I leave mom, dad, and Sasha still laughing and joking so I can begin my day and get me closer to my lunch date with Trent. I can't remember the last time I've been this happy and looking forward to a possible future with Trent. On my way to the office I stop by to see Megan to make sure she's got everything she needs. Megan was excited about her date night with her husband. Megan's parent's in-law are watching the kids for Megan and Matt tonight. She's planned to cook Matt his favorite supper and a movie. That was always their favorite things to do together. They haven't had a lot of alone time with two kids and jobs. Megan noticed that I was extremely cheerful this morning and wanted to know if it had to do with Trent. I gave her a quick rundown of the events because her client arrived early for his appointment. I hugged Megan and let her know I hoped she had a wonderful evening with Matt. She returned the hug and wished me a good day.

I've been in my office for a while now. I'm amazed that I have been able to actually get any work done. I keep catching myself daydreaming about Trent. Ashley is off today so I was able to distract myself for a little while as I was going over everything that Michelle needed to take care of today as we prepare for our meeting with Liz. I think we're prepared but I wanted to review our notes just to make sure. I haven't been keeping up with the time with the hope it would fly by. I did take a few minutes this morning when I got to my office to call down to the dining room and reserve a table for lunch. I thought it would be nice to sit on the deck overlooking the beach. While reviewing the notes I thought a few more questions to ask Liv. As I'm writing down my last question I hear my office door open. I forgot I asked Michelle to close the door on her way out earlier. Michelle would be the only one that would need me so I don't look up from what I'm doing when I speak to her. "Michelle is there something I can help you with?" "I was just thinking how sexy you look while you're working." Was the response I got but it wasn't Michelle that responded. I look up to see Trent leaning against the door he just shut. I put the pen down next to the paper I was writing on, lean back in my chair, and smile at Trent as I respond to his comment. "Let's talk about sexy. You look delicious leaning against the door." I get up from my chair as he moves away from the door. We meet in the middle of the space between my desk and door. He reaches out and wraps his arms around my waist to pull me up against him.

"I've been thinking about this all morning. It made it hard to complete my work this morning." He say just before I feel his lips against mine. The kiss starts off slow and sweet but turns into a passionate kiss. I break the kiss and lay my head on his shoulder. "I've also had a hard time working too this morning. So I totally understand." I tell him. "Glad to know I'm not the only one that has been affected." He states with a laugh. "I was finally able to complete my work and couldn't wait any longer to see you. I'm a little early for lunch. Hope you don't mind that I let myself in. There wasn't anyone at the reception desk." Trent tells me as he hugs me closer. "I don't mind at all. I wouldn't look at the clock just so I wouldn't see how slow time was passing. I was just finishing up when you walked in. I've already reserved us a table on the deck with a view overlooking the beach. The table will be held until we get there so we can go anytime we're ready." I tell him as I give him a quick kiss on the lips. "That sounds really nice. When I left my room it was about eleven o'clock. It's a beautiful day. If you're ready we'll go and enjoy an early lunch and the beautiful day all at the same time. But the best part will be spending it with you." Trent says while he's placing quick kisses on my lips and cheeks. "Yes, that does sound like a great lunch. I'm ready when you are." I reply with a laugh as he turns around to open the door. "Ladies first." He instructs as he's opening the door and just as I step in front of him he pops me on the butt. It causes me to laugh and swat at his hand but he's too quick. He laughs at my attempt. I love to see the sparkle in his eyes when he laughs. It lights up his whole face.

Chapter 21

Trent's laugh causes me to laugh at him in return. I turn back around just in time to see this beautiful tall blonde lady talking with Michelle. I could tell by her body language that she wasn't happy. The closer I got I could hear the conversation between Michelle and the lady. "Ma'am I'm sorry that I'm unable to locate the gentleman you're looking for. I can't find anyone staying here by that name." Michelle is saying. "I know he's staying here. I've spoken to him several times over the past few days he's been here." The lady replies to Michelle but continues talking before Michelle can respond. "He may have registered under his middle name instead of his first name. Check again and see if you have a Trent Hudson instead of Xzavier Hudson?" The blonde's statement causes me to stop in my tracks. Who is the beautiful lady and why is she looking for Trent. The beautiful blonde hasn't noticed me or Trent yet. Trent is still hidden behind me. Just then I noticed that Trent has come up beside me but he isn't looking at the reception desk. His attention is still on me. I know the minute he sees the lady standing at the desk. Shit is the only words I hear him say. Just about that time the lady standing at the desk turns and sees us coming up the hallway. She's more beautiful than I first thought. This women is supermodel beautiful.

"See there he is. I told you he was staying here." I hear the lady say to Michelle before she walks over to meet us. She was beautiful from the side view but once you see her completely she's stunning. Trent and I keep walking and meet her halfway down the hall way. She comes to a stop in front of Trent. "Surprise!" She says to him as she leans over and kissed him. I've never been the jealous type but seeing her kissing him is making me see red. She takes a step up, stands next to Trent, and links her arm with his. I stand there wondering who is this women and why does she think she has the right to kiss or hang onto Trent. As if she just noticed me she looks me in the eyes and extends her hand as if she would like to shake my hand. "Hi my name is Samantha Phillips, Xzavier's fiancée. It's nice to meet you." She says as we shake hands. "It's nice to meet you Ms. Phillips. I'm Sheyenne Anderson, the Event Manager for The Bed & Breakfast." I release her hand so she can't feel me shaking. I'm surprised my voice stayed so natural. I stay focused on Samantha as she turns to face Trent. "Xzavier, the lady at the desk keep telling me you weren't here." Her statement to Trent was more of a question than a statement so I answer her before Trent has a chance. "Sorry about that Ms. Phillips. When Mr. Hudson contacted my dad about staying here a few days we were completely booked. So my dad allowed him to say in one of the guest rooms in my parents living quarters that are here in the main house. With that being the case we didn't register him as quest at The Bed & Breakfast. That's why Michelle was unable to locate him in the guest registrar." I'm not sure how I'm able to sound so calm when my thoughts and heart are racing ninety to nothing. Trent is engaged to this beautiful woman but he's been sleeping with me and telling me he loved me. I take a minute to look at the two of them. She's flawless with her sky blue eyes, shoulder length blonde hair, and a tan supermodel body. "Call me Sam. That was very kind of your dad. Nikki told me how beautiful this place was. She's very excited about having her wedding here. Nikki's wedding and the location will be all anyone is talking about for the next two months. I've heard that several magazines are bidding on the rights to have an exclusive." She tells me just as I see Trent remove his arms from her hands and slides it around her waist. She leans closer and I can tell this motion was done more out of habit. Trent doesn't even look as if he's noticed what he's done. Samantha doesn't even stop talking as she wraps her arm around his waist. Trent has been looking at me the whole time Samantha and I have been talking but I will not make eye contact with him. He is smiling but it doesn't reach he eyes like it normally does. "I'm excited to hear that. Well I hate to hold you two up since you've just go here Sam. I have a few things to take care of. Sam please enjoy your time here and get Xzavier to take you for a walk on the beach at sunset. It's really beautiful. Also please enjoy lunch on the deck overlooking the beach. My sister is an amazing chief and the view is breath taking." I tell her as I turn to complete the short walk to the reception desk where Michelle is sitting. I turn without speaking to Trent but I hear Samantha's soft thanks. Just as I stop next to Michelle, Trent and Samantha walk past but I do not look up because I do not want Trent to see the pain in my eyes. I will not cry or show the emotions that are going on inside me.

Once I can no longer hear Samantha's bubbly voice I turn my attention to Michelle. "Michelle, please call down to the restaurant and make sure they're aware the table I reserved for today will be used by Mr. Hudson and his guest. Once that is done please call Liz's assistant and confirm her travel plans. Let her assistant know I'll personally pick Liz up at the dock in the morning. I'm getting ready to leave for the rest of the day so once you have the travel plans please email them to me. I'll check my email on my phone. If anyone other than family comes looking for me you are not to tell them that where I am. I'm going to Madison for the rest of the afternoon. Call or text me if you need anything else." I tell her as I'm turning to leave the reception desk. "Yes, ma'am." Michelle replies. I have so many thoughts running through my head that I'm not completely concentrating on where I'm going. My body takes over on autopilot. I leave the main house heading to my house. God she was gorgeous. I should have known he would have a girlfriend. Before I realize it I've made it to my house. I keep fighting back the tears from the hurt and pain. Why didn't he tell me he was engaged? Was he lying this morning when he told me he was in love with me? I thought I could see the truth in his eyes when he said he loved me. The hurt turns from pain to anger at how stupid I'm feeling right now. I shut down the thoughts of Trent and Samantha so I can get everything together for my stay in Madison tonight. I normally stay with either Megan or Jasper. Megan would help me sort through this mess but she already has plans with Matt. Jasper isn't home but I have a key to his house. He's told me in the past that I'm more than welcome to stay at his house anytime I needed to. I think Jasper's place would be the best place. Now that I know where I'm staying, I grab my overnight bag and start filling it with clothes for tomorrow. I'll only need clothes since I'm staying at Jasper's. Even thought Jasper and I aren't a couple he keeps the bathroom stocked with the toiletries I use for when I do stay with him.

As I'm getting everything together I call down to the dock and ask Bob to get the small boat ready for me. I'll drive it to the dock in Madison and Lance will dock it in our personal boat house. Liv and I will take the fairy from Madison to the Island in the morning so she can get the complete experience. Since cars aren't allowed on the island all cars are left at the dock. Several years ago we decided to redo the parking at the dock by putting in security cameras and a security fence. Everyone in the family has a personal car that is stored in the family car garage attached to the boat house. About three years ago we decided that adding a dock security guard would add to the security since we have people traveling to and from the island at all times of the night. I have everything that I will need for tonight and tomorrow morning. Just before I walk out of the house, I send mom, dad, and Sasha a quick text message letting them know I'm staying at Jasper's and that I'll meet Liv in the morning. I grab my overnight bag and head for the dock. Bob is just finishing his check of the boat as I come to a stop next to him. "Hi Bob, how are you today. Is the boat ready?" I ask as I through my bag in the seat. "Good afternoon, young lady. It's been a beautiful day. Yes ma'am it's ready to go. Do you want me to drive you today?" He replies as he turns to face me. "Are you okay dear?" His question catches me off guard. I thought I was hiding my feelings. "Thanks Bob but I'll drive myself today. It's been a long morning but I'll be fine. Thanks for asking." I say as I pat him on the back. "Be careful on the way into Madison. I've already called ahead and Lance is expecting you. Lance said he'd have the car pulled out of the garage for you as well." He told me as he put his hand out to help me into the boat. I lean in and give him a kiss on the cheek before I completely step into the boat. "Have great evening Bob. I won't be back until tomorrow morning." Bob nodes his head in response to my statement as he walks to untie the rope securing the boat to the dock. He's finishes the last rope just as I turn the key to start the engine. The engine starts and I slowly pull away from the dock. With a quick wave back to Bob letting him know everything is okay, I push the throttle little farther and I start my short boat ride to Madison.

Before I know it I've made it to Madison and getting in my car for the drive to Jasper's. Jasper lives just out of town. He bought a beautiful old beach house and renovated it. When he was done the beautiful old beach house was turned into the magnificent modern beach house but it still has the peaceful feel of the original old beach house. One of my favorite things in the house happens to be the master shower. Jasper's shower was the inspiration for my shower at home. The master shower has a clear glass front and doors. The glass will frost over once the steam from the shower builds up. The shower itself has three shower heads and a huge overhead shower head. You can decide how many shower heads to run at a time because each one has its own control. The shower itself can fit about four people and still have room. I picked at Jasper the first time I saw the shower. I asked him if he planned to have a party in the shower. Jasper just laughed and shook his head. He told me the only party he was having in there would be a two person party that only involved him and I. Let's just say that night we got to have that party. I'm trying to keep my thoughts on everything else so I will not think about Trent and Samantha. I've got to keep it together til I'm safely at Jaspers. The drive only takes about fifteen minutes and if you didn't know the dirt path was a driving you would miss it. Once you get past the few trees that are planted at the road so the house can't been seen, the drive opens up and you have a great view of the house and the beach. Since Jasper is gone I'll have to use the car garage door opener he gave me. Normally Jasper's here and he leaves it open for me.

I grab my keys, bag, and shut the garage door as I let myself in the house. I've always felt at home here. I take my sandals off to leave them in the mud room before I continue on to the bedroom to put my stuff away. Normally the view from the bay window in the living room would cause me to stop and enjoy the view but today I'm can't enjoy that view when my heart is breaking. I think a hot shower will help me relax. I put my bag on the bed and head for the bathroom. I get undress once I turn on the overhead shower head and one of the other ones. As I'm getting undress I feel the tears I've been holding since Samantha showed up start running down my face. I don't try to hold them back any longer. I step under the hot water and let it rain down on me as I start to cry harder. I lean my head against the cool tile wall hoping it would distract me from the feel of my heart breaking. I'm not sure how long I've been standing here crying and beating myself up for believing I could have my happy ever after with Trent

but I'm glad Jasper installed a big enough hot water heater.
The water is just as warm as it was when I first got in the
shower. I lift my head up so the water can wash the salty
tears off my face. Just then I hear the shower door open
and I turn to see Jasper standing there. "Hi Jasper, I
thought you were gone or I would have called to see if it was
okay for me to stay here tonight." I say as I start to turn
the water off. "You don't have to get out if you're not
finished yet. You also know you're welcome to stay here
anytime you need to. Are you okay? I thought I heard you
crying. That's why I open the door without knocking first."
He asks as he props against the shower door. I love Jasper
but I'm not in love with him the way I am with Trent. If I
could let go of the dream that I could be with Trent, Jasper
would be the person I would be with. I guess now that it's
clear that I can't have Trent I should let that dream go and
give it a chance with Jasper. I let my eyes travel up and
down Jasper as he stands there. Damn he's sexy in the
polo work short that isn't too tight to where his muscles
bulge out and not to lose to hide his sexy chest muscles. I
already know that his Levis fit him perfectly. I notice that
he has taken his work boots off and he's barefooted. I raise
my eyes back to meet his and answer his question. "It's
just been a very long day. I guess I'm stressed out with big
wedding that's happening at the Bed & Breakfast in two
months. I'm meeting the wedding planner tomorrow
morning so she can tour the island and discuss what needs
to be done for the wedding. Sorry for not letting you know I

was staying. I thought you were out of town for two months." "You know you're welcome here anytime. I was leaving but I got a call for another project here in town that I needed to bid on. I was leaving today after I finished the bid. I came back home to pack my suite cases to leave this afternoon but finding you here was terrific surprise. Maybe I can help relieve some of your stress?" He says with a cocky grin. Sleeping with Jasper right now would be wrong. I'll be it doing for all the wrong reasons but maybe I should use Jasper to help me forget Trent. "Would you like to join me?" I ask as I walk toward him. His eyes up until now had stayed on my face but as I walk to him fully naked he surveys me from head to toe and then back up. When his eyes meet mine again I see his hunger for me and that's what I need right now. I don't give him time to answer before I press my wet naked body to his and kiss his rough lips. Since he works out in the weather his lips are a little rougher than.... I stop myself before I can finish that thought. I will not think about him while I'm with Jasper.

Jasper deepens the kiss and pulls me tighter up against him. I grab a hold of his shirt and pull it free from the top of his pants. Jasper removes his hands from my back to grab his shirt. He breaks our kiss so he can pull it off and I hear it land on the floor next to the shower. Next he undoes his blue jeans and I hear them hit the floor as well. He steps completely into the shower and shuts the door behind him. "Turn around let me wash your hair to help you relax." He tells me as he guides me back under the spray of water. "Thank you." I reply as I hand him the shampoo. The feel of his hands massaging my head as he washes my hair feels amazing. I can feel the stress of the day start to leave me. "Hand me your body soap?" He asks and it pulls me out of my dream state. I hand it to him as he asked. He slowly starts by rubbing his hands on my neck and shoulders. The slow steady circles are helping release the tension I didn't realize was there. The slow movement of his hands down my back, around my sides, and over my breast causes me to sigh. "I'll take it by that sigh you're enjoying your bath." He whispers in my ear as he continues to knead my breast. He moves his hands back down my stomach to my hips. "Turn around and face me?" I turn to face him as he requested. The smile I see on his face warms my heart. I lay my hands on Jasper's shoulders so I can steady myself as I ask. "Pick me up?" I feel the muscles in his arms flex as he picks me up. I wrap my legs around his waist. "Now help me relieve the last little bit of stress I have left." I tell him just as he starts to walk forward. I feel the cool tiles on my back when Jasper leans down to kiss me. "It will be my pleasure to assist you." He says just as I feel him enter me. The feeling causes us both to moan with pleasure. He takes a moment before he begins to move. As he begins to move in and out of me I wrap my hands around his neck and kiss him passionately. I use the legs to help lift me as he's pulling out of me and we begin moving in rhythm together. Jasper takes my right nipple between his lips with gently sucks as he kneads my left one with his hand. I'm close and need Jasper to move harder and faster. "Jasper, harder and faster I'm so close." I moan and try to catch my breath. His only response to my request was his hands grabbing my ass to move me with his thrust. The feeling of him filling me deep and the sounds he making every time he slides in and out are driving me crazy. My orgasm hits me before I realize it. I lay my head back against the wall and moan loud enough that it bounces off the walls. Jasper doesn't stop the motion of pounding in and out of me. Pushing my orgasm on to the point where I wasn't sure it was every going to stop. "Damn you feel good sliding over my hard cock. Feeling you come undone and gripping me is sending me closer to my release." Just as Jasper finishing talking, his movements came faster and harder sending him over the edge for the first time and me for a second time.

I lay my head on Jasper's shoulders and he continues to hold me not pulling himself out of me. He steps back so we're both under the shower and I'm surprised that the water is still warm. I turn my head just enough so I can kiss Jasper's neck. I kiss a path up to his ear to whisper. "I can say you've outdid yourself. I'm completely relaxed to the point I'm not sure if my legs will work." With each kiss I can feel his semi-hard cock twitch and begin to get harder. "I'll be happy to carry wherever you want to go as long as I can stay inside you." Jasper said as he's turning the showers off. He turns toward the shower door. He has one hand wrapped around my back holding me to him as he walked. With each step he's was rubbing me. He is getting harder and I can feel another orgasm building. "I'm perfectly happy with that idea." I say breathlessly. I arch my back so I can squeeze the water from my hair. Jasper stops his movements and takes my breast in his mouth. The coolness of the air caused my nipples to harden and he's slowly sucking it. He lets go of it when I finish squeezing out my hair. He steps out of the shower reaches for the towel I left near the shower and begins drying me off. When he's done with my back I reach for the towel so I can do the same to him. I start to unwrap my legs from his waist so I can stand but he stops me. "Don't move. I'm carrying you." He tells me with a wicked grin. "Okay, I can tell by that wicked grin you're up to something. I'll be more than happy to stay on for the ride." I tell him as I slightly move hips. He laughs back as he turns to leave the bathroom. Jasper surprises me when he doesn't walk us over to the bed as we leave the bathroom. Instead he walks toward the door that leads to the porch attached to the master bedroom. He knows I love it out there. The porch overlooks a private beach that was included in the purchase of the house. He told me the beach was one of the main reasons he bought the house. Jasper turns to walk to the bench swing that's big enough for two people lay down. The cushions are thick and comfortable. I've taken several naps on this swing during the summer.

Jasper turns so he can sit down with me sitting on his lap. The swing is wide enough that Jasper can slide back stretch his legs out without them hanging over the edge. When he's finished moving himself I unhook my legs to straddle his legs. I place my hands on the back of the swing so I can position myself comfortably on Jasper's lap. I slowly start moving my hips in slow rhythm. I lean down toward Jasper to kiss him softly on the lips. As soon as our lips touch he slides his hands into my hair gently combing his fingers through it. I continue kissing him until he finishes running his fingers through my hair. I stop kissing him pull back and tell him. "Thank you for knowing what I needed." "Shy, I've always told you that I'd be here and help you any way I can." He replies between the soft kisses he's placing on my cheeks. I begin riding him a little faster and he matches my movement. Our movements cause the swing to move back and forth. We get lost in each other and we don't leave that swing until the sun starts setting. At some point we laid down and I feel asleep. I wake with Jasper holding me close to him. "Hi sleepy head." He says. "Hi, how long did I sleep?" I ask. "I'm not sure when we actually laid down but the sun has started setting. What would you like to eat for supper?" He asks. "What do you have? I would like to stay in. Tomorrow is going to be a long day since we're meeting with Liv Kross. Liv is the wedding planner for our newest client. The wedding is two months away and will be considered the highest profile wedding we've ever had. Nikki's mother is a well known designer so I'm expecting the wedding will be shown in several different magazines and TV shows. Mom and dad have worked really hard so Sasha and I are trying to insure we continue their hard work. We've got to make sure everything goes great." I say with a sigh. "I know everything will work out great. This wedding will be amazing and because of that fact the Bed & Breakfast will receive more business. I'll go see what I can throw together for supper. You can lay out here if you want and I'll bring it out to you." He tells me as he pushes up to slide over me. He and I have been out here all afternoon long. We haven't even gotten dressed. Jasper gives me a quick kiss on the cheek and slides off the swing. I pop him on the ass as he gets up. He has such a sexy ass. I love to see him walk around naked. His body is toned and tight because of the manual labor his job requires. Jasper doesn't have to work at the job sites but he prefers to. By working closely with his employees he builds trust and confidence that his men are doing a great job. "If it wasn't for the fact that we needed to eat, I wouldn't let you get up till sometime tomorrow morning." Jasper tells me over his shoulder as he gets off the swing and walks toward the door. I smile at that thought. This is exactly what I needed to keep myself from thinking about Trent. Jasper should be the one that I should be in a relationship with. I care for him and I know he cares for me. He'll love and take care of me. I've got to stop thinking about a guy I'll never have a future with.

I should get up and help Jasper with supper. I slide off the swing and walk toward the door that will take me into the bedroom where I left my bag. I decide to put on Jasper's shirt that was hanging in his closet instead of putting on any of my clothes. I put on is Jasper's shirt that hangs to bout mid-thigh. I make my way through the house to the kitchen and I see Jasper standing in the refrigerator grabbing stuff out to make hamburgers. He also stopped long enough to put on a pair of running shorts. I stop at the kitchen island and take a seat at the bar. "Sorry I ruined your plans to leave today for the job in Mississippi. I know how important it is for you to be there with your men on the different job sites." I tell Jasper. "You didn't ruin anything. Mike wasn't expecting me for a couple of more days. By me leaving today I would have been there early. Spending the afternoon with you is something I would be happy to do every day. I can still get up in the morning and head out. So tell me what you would like on your hamburger." He tells me. I stay seated at the bar while Jasper cooks the hamburgers and fixes my plate when there done cooking. For the rest of the evening Jasper and I sit around talking and joking about so many different things that time passes by quickly. Before we knew it, it's ten o'clock at night and I need to get some rest for tomorrow. Jasper sets the alarm so we both can get up at five in the morning. We plan to go for a run on the beach before we get ready for the day. I slide into bed after him and he pulls me up against him so we can snuggle together.

Chapter 22

I don't look at my cell phone until Jasper and I finish our shower after our run. There are several missed calls and texts from mom and Sasha. I send both of them quick texts letting them know I'm fine and that I will be back as soon as Liv arrives this morning. I check my emails. Michelle sent an email letting me know she confirmed that Liv should be here by eleven this morning. While I was on my phone checking emails to make sure nothing important needs my attention this morning, Jasper cooked breakfast for us. "It smells good, what are you cooking?" I ask as I sit down on the bar stool. "I've fixed a bacon and cheese omelets, buttered toast and grits." He tells me as he slides a plate in front of me. He's also fixed a cup of coffee for me. I have no doubt that it will be exactly the way I like it. "Thank you, everything looks great. What time are you leaving this morning? Liv isn't scheduled to be here until eleven. I was going to choose the furniture for the cabin while I was in town. Do you want to join me?" I ask. "I'm planning to leave about lunch time. I've already spoke to Mike this morning and everything is on schedule. Jack tells me the cabin turned out beautifully and is completely finished. I can't wait to see it. Yes, I'll join you this morning. We had such a great time planning the cabin that I can't wait to see the finished product." He answers as he sits on the bar stool next to me. We chat while we eat. When we're done I clean up both our plates and put them in the dishwasher. Japer gives me a kiss on the cheek before he goes to the bedroom to get dressed. I finish the kitchen and head to the bedroom to get ready for the day.

Jasper and I spent most of the morning picking out furniture for the cabin. One of the main items I wanted for the back porch was the bed swing like Jasper has. We laughed and joked all morning long. By the time we finished and setup delivery dates it was ten o'clock and I needed to head over to the dock just in case Liv showed up earlier. Jasper walks me to my car, opens the door and gives me a kiss. "Be careful driving. Let me know that you've made it safely." I tell Jasper. "I'll do my best to stay safe. I'll let you know how my drive is going. I want to know how great the meeting went with Liv. I know you and Sasha will do a great job." He tells me with one last kiss before he shuts my door. I wave to him as I pull out of the parking space. The drive to the dock isn't a long drive but it allows my mind time to think about Trent. Being with Jasper last night and this morning helped keep me from thinking about Trent. I can't allow myself to get upset so I force myself to concentrate on the meeting with Liv today. I can screw up this meeting if I allow myself to think about Trent and become an emotional wreck before the meeting. I begin running through the items we have to cover with Liv. Before I realize it, I'm pulling through the gate to the secure parking lot at the dock. Lance is sitting in the security office at the gate entrance. I pull to the back of the parking lot to the family's personal parking. I glance at the clock to see its fifteen after ten. Liv should be in within the next forty five minutes so I'll spend that time talking with Michael. Michael is our head security officer and has been working on the updates to our current security.

Michael had just finished showing me last of his plans for updating the parking lot security system when Lance announced over the intercom that Liv has just arrived. I had already arranged for Lance to direct Liv's driver to park in one of the extra family parking spaces. I wish Michael a good day and tell him thanks for all of his hard work on the security system. By the time I make it over to greet Liv, her drive is opening the back driver side door. A beautiful petit middle aged woman exited the car and then a younger lady who was just as beautiful exited behind her. I'm guessing that Liv also brought her assistant with her. I walk over so I can introduce myself. "Good morning, I'm Sheyenne Anderson. It's a pleasure to meet you." I say as I extend my hand. The middle aged woman takes my hand to shake it. "Good morning,

Sheyenne. It's a pleasure to finally meet you. I'm Liv Kross and this is my daughter and assistant Alley." She tells me as she is letting my hand go. "It is a pleasure to finally meet you in person. If you will follow me, I have a boat ready to take us to the island." I decided not to take the fairy this morning but to instead take the boat back. Liv turns and gives her driver instructions before we start the short walk to the boating dock. During our short walk to the dock, I explained the boat schedule for the passenger boat that carries guest to and from the island. I also let her know we have a boat that is specifically used to carry supplies to the island. This boat would be used to carry any equipment she had to bring for the wedding.

Nathan was waiting for us when we reached the boat. Before we could climb aboard he was handing us each a life vest. Once the life vest was secure he helped us aboard the boat. "Thanks Nathan." I told him as he was walking to the front of the boat. "You're welcome ma'am. I'll untie the boat from the dock once you're ready to go." He tells me as he bends down at the first rope. I start the small boat and wait for Nathan to finish untying the last rope. I wave to Nathan once more as we slowly pull away from the dock. "You can handle this boat very well." Alley states. "Yes, dad thought it was a necessity that Sasha and I know how to operate a boat. He started teaching us at a very young age how to operate different types of boats. We can actually drive several different types of boats and a few other watercrafts. This one is fairly small but it is one of my favorite ones to drive." I tell her before I turn my attention back to the water. Both ladies commented on how beautiful the day is. We chatted about their drive to Madison. As we were pulling up to the dock on the island, I was telling Liv how beautiful the scenery will be based on the time Nikki has chosen for the wedding. Bob is waiting for us on the dock so he can tie the boat dock. "Good morning Bob. Thank you for your help. How are you doing this morning?" I ask as I switch off the boat and motion for Liv and Alley to exit the boat. "Morning Sheyenne and good morning to you as well ladies." Bob reaches out to assist Liv, then Alley and lastly me out of the boat and onto the dock. Once we handed Bob our life vest, we start the walk to the main house. Just as we pass the boat house Sasha steps out to meet us. We come to a stop in front of Sasha as I begin to introduce her. "Liv. Alley. This is my sister Sasha. Sasha, this is Liv and her daughter and assistant Alley." They each shake each other's hand. "If you would like to follow me, I have lunch ready on the back deck. Mom and dad are meeting us there." Sasha tells us as she turns to walk toward the main house. Liv and Alley talk back and forth about how beautiful the walk to the house is. "I love the house." Liv says as the house comes into view. "Thank you; this is the original house our grandparents built when they first opened the Bed and Breakfast sixty years ago. Over the years updates have been made but the original structure wasn't changed." I finish saying just as we make it to the dining room. "Hi

Caroline, has mom and dad made it yet?" I hear Sasha ask as we walk in the waiting area. "Yes, ma'am they came through here about five minutes ago." Caroline answered. "Thank you." I reply as I pass her.

Mom and dad are standing at the railing looking out at the beach. "Hi mom and dad, this is Liv and Alley Kross. Liv. Alley. This is our parents John and Lilly Anderson." I say when we come to a stop in front of mom and dad. They each say their hellos when Sasha walks up to me and gives me a questionable look. I know she wants to talk about Trent. She had to see him with Samantha. I slightly shake my head telling her I don't want to talk. We all take our seats just as Mark our waiter comes to take our drink orders. "I have to say Nikki was hundred percent correct when she stated this was a beautiful place. I can't wait to see the wedding and reception locations." Liv is saying when Mark returns with our drinks and appetizer sampler. "I hope you don't mind but I've already ordered a variety of appetizers, main courses, and desserts." Sasha says as Mark sets everything down on the table. We eat and talk and lunch seemed to pass quickly but it was an enjoyable time. It was great to get to know everyone. We were also able to decide on the meal for Nikki's wedding rehearsal. "Liv if you would like we can walk down to the beach and then the garden so you can see the site for yourself. I know Nikki shared the photos she took but to actually see the locations doesn't even compare." I ask as we leave the deck by the stairs leading down to the walking trails. "Yes, that would be great. The photos Nikki shared were amazing. If the photos only showed half of the beauty I can't wait to see it in person." She answers as she comes beside me. I glance around and see Alley making notes as we talk about the items Liv expects for us to handle for the setup for the wedding and reception. I look over at Sasha and she is also making notes on the information we put together. By the time we make it to the beach we've worked out most of the details. "Wow this is a gorgeous beach." I hear Liv say as the beach comes into site. "Thanks I love this beach because of the sand and how the sun shines on it. I was thinking instead of using chairs for seating that white benches with a back would look great." I tell her as we walk further down the beach. "If Nikki doesn't mind and if the tide isn't high that afternoon, they could stand closer to the water in the far corner over there. That way we can set the benches up the beach." I point to the beautiful area a little ways in front of us. "Yes I agree that would be a wonderful idea." Liv says as she keeps looking around the beach area.

Liv was just as impressed with garden where the reception will be held. "Would you be against hanging small lights over the garden? I believe the small lights will add to the beauty of the garden. Those and any small candles or table lights would be the only lights in the garden. It will look like a fantasy." Liv asks when she comes to stand beside mom, dad, Sasha, and I. "I think that is a lovely idea Liv." Mom answers. "Yes, I agree that would be a great idea." I comment. "If you would like we can show you where the wedding party and the guest will be staying. There's also a cabin for Nikki and Jeremiah to spend their first night together as husband and wife." I ask. "I'd love to see it. I believe Jeremiah is planning to surprise Nikki with a trip for their honeymoon. I'll let him know to plan to leave the next day. They'll love being able to celebrate with their family longer instead of having to rush off to catch a plane." Liv tells us as we walk down the path to the new guest houses and cabin. As we get closer to the cabin the memories from my night with Trent slowly begin to surface. I see Jack standing at the entrance talking with a few of the construction crew. I haven't checked on the status in a few days. Talking with Jack will be a way of avoiding going to the cabin. I'm not sure I could hold myself together if I go to the cabin. "Let me know if Jeremiah needs anything. I'll be glad to assist in any way that I can." I tell Liv as we start walking to the cabin. "Sasha, I need to stop and talk with Jack." I say before turning to walk up the path where Jack is standing. Sasha waves to let me know she heard me. They continue walking toward the cabin.

I've just finished talking with Jack when the group is walking back past us. I thank Jack for the information as I turn to catch up with them. They're all chatting about the cabin and the beautiful view of the beach from the porch and I don't want to interrupt the conversion. I have a tight feeling in my chest as they continue to talk about the beach and how beautiful it is. Within a few minutes we've make it back to the main house. Mom and dad say their good bye to Liv and Alley. Sasha, Liv, Alley, and I continue walking to the dock. "Shy, I'll drive Liv and Alley back to Madison. I've planned to go see Lee so we can talk about the food list for the rehearsal dinner, wedding, and reception. Are you going to be okay? We haven't had a chance to talk about what has happened." Sasha comes up beside me while Liv and Alley walk a few feet in front of us. Liv and Alley are in the middle of their own conversion. "Sure no problem. Please let me know you've made it to Savannah. I'll be fine. We'll talk when you get back." I tell her as we make it to the dock. Sasha walks in the boat house and comes back out with her suitcase. Bob is waiting for us at the boat. He takes the suitcase form Sasha and places it in the boat. "Sheyenne. Sasha. I'm excited to be working with you. I think this will be a great partnership for the both of us."

Liv states as Bob helps Alley on the boat. "Thanks Liv. We're excited as well to be working with you." I tell her as I shake her hand. "My nephew was correct when he told me how beautiful it was here." She says as Bob begins to help her on the boat. "Sorry I didn't know your nephew has stayed here." I say. I was a little confused by her statement. "I should have known he won't say anything. Yes, he's been here almost a week now. I've spoken to him several different times while he's been here. He's told me how nice everyone has been. I know you've met my nephew because he said your dad was nice enough to allow him to stay in the private living area." She said just as she takes her sit on the boat. Bob had placed a life vest on the seat for each of them. Sasha turns to look at me as I say. "Xzavier Hudson is your nephew." Luckily neither Liv nor Alley saw the look that Sasha gave me. Sasha turns back to face them as Liv looks back at me. I did my best to keep my voice level. I've done the best I could to keep from thinking about Trent today. "Yes he is. His dad is my brother. Once we get back to New York, I'll have Alley type up our notes and send them to you for review. It was a pleasure meeting you and spending the afternoon with you and your parents. I think this is going to be the beginning of a terrific partnership." Liv tells us as she finishes getting seated for the ride back to Madison. "It's be a pleasure for us a well. I'll work on our notes and sent them over for your review as well. Hope you have a safe trip home. Sasha, please call to let us know you've made it safely to Savannah." Bob has just finished untying the last rope when I finish talking to them. Sasha starts the engine and gives me a thumb up to let me know she heard me. I stand there for a few minutes watching them ride off.

Chapter 23

I take my time walking back to my house. It's been a long past couple of days and I don't want to take the chance that I might run into Trent and Samantha. It was hard keeping my cool yesterday and I don't think I could today. I was counting on distancing myself from him until the wedding but with Liv being his aunt. I'm pulled away from my thoughts by the sound of my phone going off. I realize that I have just received a text. I know it couldn't be Sasha, she just left. I pull my phone from my pocket, take a quick glance up and notice I'm on the path that takes me up to my front porch. I keep walking up the path while I check my phone to see who has text me. It's a message from Jasper. I smile because his text couldn't have come at a better time. He wants to know how well the meeting went and to let me know it's been an uneventful drive. He's stopping to eat and get a room for the night. I don't look up from my phone when I make it to the hand railings attached to the front porch steps. I lean up against the railing while I text Jasper back letting him know the meeting went well and I was glad his drive has been safe.

"It must be good news." I'm surprised to hear someone speak. I jerk my head up quickly to see Trent sitting in the rocking chair on the porch. "Yes, it is. What are you doing here? Shouldn't you be busy showing your fiancé around the island?" I say but I'm unable to hold the sharpness in my voice. I walk up the few steps to come to a stop on the porch. Trent gets up from the chair and walks over to me. He stops a few feet in front of me. "I'm sorry you found out about her like that. That's what I've been wanting to talk to you about. I'm not in love with Samantha. I've never been in love with her." Trent starts telling me but I hold my hand up stopping him mid speech. "Trent, I don't want to hear whatever story you feel you have to tell me. We had a great few nights and days. Let's leave it that way." It's killing me to tell him that because I've loved him so long. "You and I both know what's going on between us is more than just a couple of nights and days. I'm in love with you and have been since the first time we met five years ago. I just need time to deal with Samantha." He steps a little closer as he continues to speak to me. I can hear sounds of people walking up the path to the house. The sounds of laugher are getting louder and then I hear. "Mama." "Mama." "I see mama." The beautiful laughing voices cause Trent to stop. A look of shock and confusion shows in Trent's eyes.

Just as I turn around Alexis and TJ come running up the stairs. I squat so I can give them both a big hug. I've missed them this week. There were away at camp. Brandy is a nurse and she helps out at both camps that Alexis and TJ went to. Alexis went to Camp Little Shot. Camp Little Shot is a camp for children with Type 1 Diabetes. Alexis was diagnosed last year shortly after her fourth birthday. So Brandy thought it would be a great idea for Alexis to go to Camp Little Shot and meet other kids just like her. There are kids of all ages that go to the weeklong camp. The camp is free for kids to attend. It is run off the donations it receives and the hard work of the volunteers who help out. TJ went to Camp Little Support. Camp Little Support is for the siblings of the children attending Camp Little Shot. At Camp Little Support the kids learn about the disease their siblings have and what they can do to help their brother or sister. This camp is also run on donations and the volunteers who help out. Alexis and TJ are standing in front of as I stay squatted down to be eye level with them. "Hi sweethearts. Mama has missed y'all. Did you have fun at camp?" I ask both kids. They haven't paid attention to Trent standing there yet. They're excited to see me. "Yesss ma'am. There was sooo many like me there. Some took shots. Others had this little box. We got to swim and play a lot." Alexis answered with waving hands. She's my dramatic child. "Sounds like you had a great time Alexis. So TJ did you have a great time at camp?" I say as I turn to face TJ. He's standing there so calmly will Alexis bounces around. "Yes, ma'am. It was fun." He replied. About that time TJ noticed that Trent was standing there watching us. "Mama whose he?" He asks as he points his small finger up at Trent. Alexis turns around and gives Trent a big smile. "This is Mr. Hudson. He's a guest here." I tell them. Trent is looking at me and then back and forth at the kids. I can see the questions in his eyes but instead of asking them he squats down and sticks his hand out at TJ. "Hi TJ, you can call me Trent if you like." Trent says to TJ. TJ slightly shakes his hands before he lets go. Trent then turns to Alexis. "Hi Alexis." Trent extends his hand as he talks to her but instead of taking his hand she gives him a big hug that he returns.

"Alright you two little rug rats. You left me carrying your stuff." Brandy says as she starts up the steps. Before she can say anything else she sees Trent hugging Alexis and gives me a glance before she finishes her statement. "Come here and get the small bags and carry them in the house." Alexis lets go of Trent and turns her laughing blue eyes to Brandy. "Bandy, I love you." Alexis bounces over to Brandy. "I love you too squirt but that isn't going to get you out of carrying the bag." Brandy tells her as she hands Alexis the bag. TJ comes up beside Alexis to get his bag. "Hi Shy, I'll take the kids inside and get them settled down and ready for baths." She tells me as leads the kids to the front door. "Bye Alexis. Bye TJ. It was really nice meeting you." Trent says as he stands back up. Both kids wave bye as they walk into the house. As soon as the door shuts, Trent turns to face me. I'm preparing myself for his questions.

"So how old are they?" Is his first question. "They'll be five in September." With my answer I can see him doing the math in his head. "So I see you held information back from me as well. When were you going to tell me?" I can't tell if his voice if filled with hurt or anger. He seems to be holding his feelings in check. "I told you that I needed to talk with you but we kept putting it off. I was going to talk with you before you left." I replied. "So if I hadn't showed up here today and they happened to come home were you going to tell me?" He asks. "I'm not sure what I would have done but I'm not going to have this discussion now. I need to get inside and help with them." I say as I take a few steps toward the front door. "I'm leaving tonight as soon as I leave here. I'm going straight to the dock, there's a boat waiting to carry me back to Madison. Goodbye Nicole." He says as he walks off the porch. "Goodbye Trent." I finish saying as I shut the front door. I lean against the door once I've shut it. "So is that who I think it was?" Brandy asks. I open my eyes and look at Brandy. "Yes that was Trent, Alexis and TJ's dad. Let's go get them settled and I'll explain everything to you.

The End...... For Now there's more to come with Nicole and Trent

Camp Little Shot is an actual camp for kids ages 6 to 18 with Type 1 Diabetes. The camp gives the kids an opportunity to meet other kids who have the same condition. The camp is ran off the donations and is free for all kids that attend. Please take a few minutes and read more about the camp.

http://camplittleshot.com/?page_id=24

ABOUT THE AUTHOR

Misty Payton is a single mother of two kids. Her son Ricky and daughter Chelby mean to world to her. She thanks the Lord everyday for blessing her with these two amazing kids. Misty took her love of reading and decided to write the stories she loves to read.